Bello:
hidden talent rediscovered

Bello is a digital only imprint of Pan Macmillan,
established to breathe new life into previously published,
classic books.

At Bello we believe in the timeless power of the imagination,
of good story, narrative and entertainment and we want to use
digital technology to ensure that many more readers
can enjoy these books into the future.

We publish in ebook and Print on Demand formats
to bring these wonderful books to new audiences.

www.panmacmillan.co.uk/bello

T0331526

Margaret Pemberton

Margaret Pemberton is the bestselling author of over thirty novels in many different genres, some of which are contemporary in setting and some historical.

She has served as Chairman of the Romantic Novelists' Association and has three times served as a committee member of the Crime Writers' Association. Born in Bradford, she is married to a Londoner, has five children and two dogs and lives in Whitstable, Kent. Apart from writing, her passions are tango, travel, English history and the English countryside.

Margaret Pemberton

TAPESTRY
OF FEAR

BELL

First published in 1979 by Hale

This edition published 2013 by Bello
an imprint of Pan Macmillan, a division of Macmillan Publishers Limited
Pan Macmillan, 20 New Wharf Road, London N1 9RR
Basingstoke and Oxford
Associated companies throughout the world

www.panmacmillan.co.uk/bello

ISBN 978-1-4472-4469-1 EPUB
ISBN 978-1-4472-4468-4 POD

Visit **www.panmacmillan.com** to read more about all our books
and to buy them. You will also find features, author interviews and
news of any author events, and you can sign up for e-newsletters
so that you're always first to hear about our new releases.

To the memory of my mother-in-law,
Marjorie May Pemberton,
who enjoyed life even more than Miss Daventry.

Chapter One

"I have a surprise for you," Pedro said. "Miss Daventry, an Englishwoman. She is an old, old friend of mine. Whenever she is in the Basque country she stays in my inn. You will like her. She is . . ." he searched for the words, then said with a beaming smile. "She is one of your English eccentrics!"

Intrigued I followed him into the tiny inn. It only had two guest rooms, with waxed wood floors, white-walled and spartan. A single stone staircase divided the dining-room and kitchen from the bar where Pedro spent most of his time, shouting orders to Jaime, the good natured barman, and to Maria and Carmen who did the cooking and cleaning. He was a typical Basque. Large and jovial, his face the colour of tanned leather, with drooping black moustaches and a large apron tied around his ample figure. He had been overjoyed at my ability to speak Spanish and taken great pride in introducing me to the local fishermen who crammed his tiny bar.

He flung open the heavy oak door that led to the dining-room, introducing me with a flourish. Miss Daventry was easily in her seventies and looked rather formidable. She was tall and angular with a no nonsense approach about her. Wisps of steel grey hair escaped from a bun at the nape of her neck and she wore a straw boater on her head and a pair of heavy binoculars and a camera slung crosswise around her neck.

"Sit down, sit down," she said as Pedro hurried off towards the kitchen. "Really, if I'd known the man was going to make such a fuss of me I'd have given Miguelou a miss and gone to Africa instead."

"You travel a lot?" I asked, pouring myself a drink of water.

"Well of course child, what else is life for?" then, without waiting for an answer. "I've just finished touring Hungary and the Carpathian mountains, such *interesting* places still to be found in central Europe. Little villages quite cut off from the modern world. Before Hungary I visited Syria and did a little digging in Antioch. There's always something to be found there. Mosaic pavements and bits of this and pieces of that. Of course the archeologists aren't at all pleased by amateurs, I find them such a *selfish* group of people ... and there is Daphne, once so licentious and now nothing but a laid out garden. Such a pity," she said wistfully. "It must have been much more interesting before." She paused for a few minutes, absorbed in the past days of Daphne, and then said with renewed vigour: "I didn't feel like continuing down into Palestine, or Israel, or whatever else you now call it. The whole area is dreadfully spoilt, not like it used to be, but it's the same everywhere. This part of Spain for instance, hardly recognisable these days. Thank God Miguelou's been left alone, if it hadn't I'd have gone south again. Africa ... I really should visit Africa. ..."

"Pedro tells me you are old friends," I said, as the prospect of Africa clouded her eyes.

"Friends?" she said with a start. "Oh good heavens yes. I've known Pedro for years, but of course it was all a long time ago ... during the civil war. ..."

Before I could ask any more Carmen came in with two steaming plates of caldeirada. Miss Daventry beamed at her.

"So you are Antonio's daughter. Sit down while we eat and tell me how your father is keeping. Pedro tells me he is in Madrid."

Carmen nodded shyly. Miss Daventry patted the seat of a wooden chair.

"Come on, sit down, there's no need to be shy. How old are you, eighteen, nineteen?"

"Eighteen," she said, sitting down beside us.

"And what is this about Domingo? Pedro tells me he is in Carabanchel."

She didn't answer for a moment, her fingers playing with the hem of her apron, and with horror I saw that her eyes were filled with tears.

"Domingo is a politico."

"A politico?" I asked, mystified. "What does that mean?"

"A politico," Miss Daventry said, "means he is a political prisoner. Carabanchel jail is in Madrid."

I put down my fork. The caldeirada no longer tasted pleasant.

"What has your brother done?" I asked.

"He is a separatist. The police caught him distributing leaflets ..."

"ETA is the name of the Basque separatist movement. Nearly all the men in Miguelou will be members," Miss Daventry said as Carmen's tears began afresh.

"They allow him to write two letters a week," she slipped her hand and brought a creased envelope, its contents obviously read and re-read over and over again. "Perhaps soon he will be home ..." Her lips trembled and she stuffed the letter back into her pocket and hurried from the room. Silence hung heavily for a few moments and then Miss Daventry sighed: "They never give up. There was a meeting in the bar this morning and you can bet your life it was political. Pedro was cooped up with Javier Mendez, the local romeo, Alfonso Cia, the local delinquent, Angel Garmendia, the local madman, and the village priest, Father Eustacio Calzada."

"Sounds an interesting assortment. I met Javier Mendez and Angel Garmendia in the bar last night. Javier wanted to show me the night life in Zarauz, he was quite persuasive."

"Javier is all right. But have nothing to do with Garmendia. He was shot in the head two years ago during riots in Bilbao. Pedro says he has been a man to fear ever since."

"Then why was he cooped up in the bar with him this morning?"

"I don't know, but I'd like to. I'll go and have a word with him now."

I finished my wine and then followed her out of the room, going upstairs for my swimming costume. The heat was uncomfortable and I had seen a nice little bay half a mile to the north of Miguelou that looked perfect for swimming. I spent the rest of the afternoon alternately swimming and sun-bathing, completely at peace and blissfully unaware how soon that peace was to be shattered.

That night an uncanny silence hung over the inn.

"Where is everyone?" I asked at last.

"I've no idea. I couldn't get any sense out of Pedro at all. I think I'll have an early night. The feeling in the bar is distinctly inhospitable."

She was right. When I pulled the bead curtain aside the men fell silent and even Jaime was unwelcoming. Puzzled I let the curtain fall and went upstairs to my room. The monotonous rhythm of the water splashing against the harbour wall soon lulled me into a deep and dreamless sleep.

It was shattered abruptly. Out at sea there came the throb of an engine and as I padded across to the window and looked outside, I could see a speedboat racing across the bay, arc lights crossing and re-crossing the ocean. Then, just beyond Miguelou's headland, silhouetted in the searchlight, I saw the pale grey of a fishing boat ploughing through flying clouds of spray, and running figures. Above the noise of the speedboat's engine came a new, terrifying sound as gunfire ripped into the fishing boat and there came the distant sound of screams and cries. Horrified I stared as the speedboat thundered down on the fishing boat. The searchlight illuminated the scene grotesquely and I could see uniformed figures and then the curved arch of a man as he dived from the now captured fishing boat into the blackness of the sea. I cried out as a uniformed figure took aim and fired again. In the glaring ring of light another body dropped, sinking into the darkness of the water. Within minutes the fishing boat had been boarded and then the speedboat turned, its engines revving as it bore down towards the harbour.

I wrenched myself from the window, running for Miss Daventry. At the sound of my approach she wheeled round, her fingers to her lips.

"They shot them. . . ." I gasped painfully.

"Sssh," In the distance came the sound of running feet. "Into bed. *Quick!* You heard nothing and saw nothing, understand?"

"Yes," I said, understanding all too well.

4

I was trembling violently as I clambered back into my own bed, every nerve stretching to catch a new sound, a fresh movement. I heard the inn door open and the sound of harsh breathing and racing steps and I clenched my fist against my mouth. In the distance I heard the speedboat as it roared into Miguelou's harbour, and then all hell broke loose. There were shouts and screams and the sound of pounding feet and breaking glass. With difficulty I controlled my breathing as loud knocking shook the tiny inn and I heard Pedro opening the door, his voice raised in protest as the police swarmed past him, throwing open doors and mounting the stairs towards the bedrooms.

My door was flung open and the brilliant glare of a torch dazzled my eyes. For a second as I sat there, the covers clutched in my hand, eyes blinking against the light, he said nothing, the torchlight swept the walls and floor and then swung back to my face.

"What is happening? What is the meaning of this?" I said in English, my voice unnaturally high.

"Your passport," he ordered curtly. Indignantly I wrapped my dressing-gown around me and walked across to where my handbag lay on the dresser. He examined it carefully and thrust it back at me. Next door Miss Daventry's voice rose loud and clear.

"How *dare* you! I am a British citizen. I shall report this to the Embassy tomorrow. Do . . . you . . . understand? The *British* Embassy. Yes, that is my passport and I will have it back please. Can the man speak no English? I am British and the Embassy will have something to say about this!"

Her voice carried on, outraged and dignified as they disappeared downstairs.

Miss Daventry said: "Stay in your room, Alison. I'll come to you in a little while."

There came the sound of Pedro bolting the door after his unwelcome guests and Miss Daventry descended the stairs, stern and resolute.

It seemed an eternity before she returned. She turned the oil lamp up and sat on the edge of the bed, her face grim.

Chapter Two

I waited. She said sombrely: "The boat trying to reach Miguelou's harbour was the reason for all the tension today. The men on board were Basque separatists trying to smuggle guns and ammunition into Miguelou from Bayonne, in France."

"To Angel Garmendia?"

"It looks like it."

"No wonder there was a strained atmosphere tonight."

"Apparently everyone was in on it, Pedro included. The idea was that the village men would distribute the weapons to all the local ETA units."

"Were any local men on board?"

"Four. Among them Luis and Jose Villada. Jose is Carmen's fiance."

My stomach turned an unpleasant somersault. "Are they dead?"

She shrugged despairingly. "No-one knows. Pedro was on the beach with the rest of the men waiting for the boat to land. He managed to escape and get back to the inn before the police arrived, but some of the others stayed, in case any survivors should reach shore. The police have arrested them all."

"And Jaime?" I asked. "Was Jaime on the beach?"

She nodded. "Pedro says he wouldn't leave, one of the men on board the boat was his cousin."

I reached for my dressing-gown.

"And where do you think you are going?"

"To Carmen."

She laid a hand on my arm restrainingly. "There is no point in going to her room, Alison. She is missing. Pedro doesn't know where she is. There is nothing we can do tonight. Try and get some sleep."

She went out, shutting the door quietly behind her. I lay in the darkness, remembering again the clarity of the man's body as it hung in agony before sinking down into the foam flecked depths of the sea. I wondered if Carmen had seen it too, and recognised it. Was that why her room was empty? Sick at heart, I turned over, burying my face in the pillow, waiting for morning.

It took a long time to come. The early morning sun slowly lightened my room, but the usual sounds from the street below were absent and the inn remained still and silent. Then I heard steps on the stone stairs, and Pedro's voice, low and dull, and I dressed hurriedly. As soon as I saw his haggard face, my heart sank.

Miss Daventry was standing beside him at the semi-circle of wood that served as his desk, she turned as I approached and said simply: "Jaime is dead."

Pedro pushed a glass into my hand, saying brokenly. "Six men have died, six . . . and the police have taken nearly every man that remains away for questioning."

"What about Javier?"

"Javier is missing. And Angel and Alphonso. Angel will be like a man demented. . . ."

"His brother was shot and killed on the beach." Miss Daventry said bluntly.

Pedro turned his back to me, leaning heavily on his desk. Miss Daventry took me by the arm.

"Someone wants to see you in the kitchen."

"Carmen? She's back?"

Miss Daventry nodded. "Yes, she's back, and refusing to talk to anyone but yourself. You had better have a word with her."

She was sat at the scrubbed table, her hands clenched tightly in her lap. She sprang to her feet as I parted the bead curtain, her face tense and strained, dark circles beneath her eyes. Her skirt was dirty and damp, the hem thick with mud, her legs scratched and bleeding. She grasped my hand urgently: "*You saw what happened?*"

"Yes. I saw everything. But where have you been?"

"Will you help me? You *must* help me. Before I tell you where I have been, promise you will help ... for if you don't there is no-one else. ..." her voice broke off in a strangled sob. "Pedro says the police know I was missing last night, that they have not arrested me because they are watching me ... wanting me to lead them to. ..." She pressed her fist to her mouth, and took a deep, steadying breath. "Please. Without your help Luis and Jose will die!"

"*They're alive?*" I asked incredulously.

She nodded. "But they are injured and I dare not go to them again, for Pedro says I will be followed."

"Where are they?"

"I can only tell if you promise to help!" I nodded, her hand gripping mine so tight that her nails dug in my flesh. "They swam ashore last night and I was waiting. I knew they were on the boat and I *had* to go down to the beach. Luis has been shot in the leg and Jose in the shoulder. While the police searched the village we crept along the beach and then took two of old Manuel's donkeys and climbed to Maria's cottage."

"You mean they are *here? In the village?*" I asked aghast.

She shook her head. "Maria only works here when Pedro needs her. She has a cottage of her own on the slopes of the mountain. Miss Daventry knows where it is. She has been there often. You must take them food and bandages. ..."

"But. ..."

"*You must!* Otherwise they will die! I will get the things now!"

"Maria. ..." but she had already gone.

Miss Daventry came in, saying: "Well?"

"Carmen's fiance and his brother are hiding in Maria's cottage."

"Good."

"It's not good at all," I said bad-temperedly. "Both of them have been shot and Carmen says it is impossible for her to go and help, or anyone else in the village, as the police would follow. And that without help they will die."

"And did Carmen have a solution?"

"Yes. That I should."

"What a sensible idea, and with me to help. . . ."

"I don't happen to have any sympathies with terrorists, Basques or otherwise."

"But the men are dying." Miss Daventry protested.

A long minute went past.

"If I go. I go alone."

"You don't know where the cottage is. . . ."

"Then you will go?" Pedro asked eagerly. I nodded and his face flushed with excitement. "Then you must speak to Father Calzada."

Minutes later the black robed priest held out a thin hand to shake.

"You are going to help us? I am grateful. If God is good, the Villada's will be in France in twenty-four hours. A boat will sail from Bayonne tonight. It will pass Miguelou and wait in the bay a little to the north. There it will pick up the Villada's."

"But if they've been shot they won't be fit to travel."

"They will have to be," the little priest's voice was firm.

"But the coastguard?"

"The launch is crewed by Germans. If they are stopped they are tourists, their passports are in order. Jose and Luis will be hidden. It is a risk but it is one that has to be taken. If they *are* found . . ." he shrugged.

"And is this the best you can come up with?" Miss Daventry asked.

"A lot of money has been spent securing the use of the boat and the men. The plan is as good as any other."

There was a general feeling of unease. The priest locked his fingers together. "It is the only way. It must be tried."

Miss Daventry frowned. "We will do our best then. But from what Carmen says the journey could be the death of them."

"If they stay," Father Calzada said quietly. "It will be the death of them."

The cottage sheltered in splendid isolation beneath the bare and shining peaks of the mountains. Miss Daventry rapped on the door and two chaffinches flew off with a flutter of wings and a trill of reproach. Nothing happened. There was no sound of movement.

"It's obvious they won't answer unless they know who is knocking," I said at last. I put my mouth as near the door as possible.

"We are friends. Carmen and Pedro have sent us with food and medical supplies."

Still there was no response. I tried again: "We are English, but we want to help you. We have come for Luis and Jose Villada."

As my words died away I could hear a slight movement from inside. Miss Daventry smiled with satisfaction. We waited expectantly. Heavy bolts at top and bottom slid back and then the door swung slowly inwards.

"What do you want?"

He was about nineteen with dark curly hair and a sullen expression on his face which did nothing to detract from his fierce good looks.

"We are friends of Carmen's. We have food and bandages."

He opened the door wider, calling over his shoulder: "Do you hear that, Jose?"

From the dark interior came a low reply and then he was ushering us into the cottage. Miss Daventry smiled triumphantly.

I was just about to speak to her when my arms were wrenched behind my back and someone unseen pulled me tightly against them. I cried out, and as I did so his hand covered my mouth. Unbelievingly I struggled, kicking with all my might, twisting to free myself from his grasp. I have a vague recollection of the look of stunned amazement on Miss Daventry's face, and then the boy who had opened the door to us, had his hand tightly over her mouth, pinioning her arms, dragging her out of the room.

From his gasps and curses it was obvious that Miss Daventry was not going easily and neither for that matter, was I. In a blind sea of rage I wrenched myself round, trying to unbalance him, anything, anything at all. . . . He swore viciously and then his hand let go of my mouth as my efforts to bite him succeeded. For one brief second I screamed and then his hand came down hard on the side of my head, sending me spinning across the stone flagged floor and smashing into the wall. My head split with pain and as I fell dizzily to the floor I saw, with distorted vision, my attacker slump down lifelessly opposite me.

Chapter Three

My head swam and the next few moments were a blur of pain and shock. I was dimly aware that there were only the two of us in the room, and that my attacker was lying unconscious and helpless. I pressed my hands against the floor, willing myself to stand, to move. . . .

The inner door swung open, and the young man, minus Miss Daventry, staggered, limping, over to the apparently lifeless body. Dazedly I watched him, trying to gather my wits and my strength. I raised myself gingerly to a sitting position and he spun round.

"You stay there, understand? If you do not move you will not be hurt."

"What have you done with my friend? Is she hurt, is. . . ."

The boy said sourly. "She is not hurt. Not yet."

"You are being very silly," I said, as the blinding pain in my head eased a little. "If you will just listen to me a minute. . . ."

"*Be quiet!*" he hissed, propping his brother against the wall, steadying him as his eyes slowly opened. Hazily they focused on me and he tried to move.

"My friend is very old. What have you done with her?"

He touched his face fleetingly and I could see deep scratches gouged the length of his cheek. Miss Daventry had certainly put up a fight, but there was no sound from her now, and a new, dreadful fear engulfed me. I called out loudly: "Miss Daventry, are you all right? Can you hear me? Miss Daventry. . . ."

The boy limped angrily across the room towards me, his face white with pain. "*Silence! Not another word.* . . ."

"Miss Daven. . . ."

He seized my arm viciously and I was too dazed to wriggle free.

"If you promise to be quiet I will show you your friend is unharmed, right?"

I nodded, and he allowed me to rise shakily to my feet, then, still held in his grip, he propelled me towards the inner door. With my heart in my mouth I stared into the dimness beyond.

Across a rough stone floor stood an iron bed, and dumped down upon it, straw hat askew, hands and feet tied with sheeting, and firmly gagged, sat the glowering figure of Miss Daventry. Heedless of the boy's protests I ran across to the bed, pulling at the hastily tied knots of the gag, saying: "Don't scream, it's going to be all right. . . ."

"Just what, my dear Alison," she said as the rag fell from her mouth, "is happening?"

"They are not as joyful to see us as you anticipated."

"Haven't you explained?" she asked as the boy eyed us warily.

"I haven't had a chance. . . . I've just had my head smashed against a wall."

"I am sure he did not mean it," Miss Daventry said optimistically. "We probably hurt them more than they hurt us."

"They were supposed to be helpless and at death's door." I said, feeling the back of my head.

"Carmen's exaggeration. I am sure he will apologise. They must have had a dreadful night. The swim ashore would have been bad enough and then the journey here . . . and both of them injured . . ."

I tried to feel suitably sympathetic and failed.

"And now young man," Miss Daventry said, turning to the boy who had been listening to us in growing bewilderment. "Please undo these knots. I cannot do anything for your leg trussed up like a Christmas turkey."

Mesmerised, he took out a knife from his belt and did as he was told. Miss Daventry smiled with gratification, then she nimbly swung her legs off the bed and rubbed her wrists.

"Allow me to introduce myself. My name is Miss Daventry, my friend here is Alison Russell, we are staying at the inn owned by

Pedro Triana in Miguelou." He backed away nervously. Miss Daventry continued undeterred. "Carmen told us of your predicament. She could not come back herself as the police have taken over the village and she was frightened she would be followed. Apparently one of your half drowned friends gave your names when arrested, and as your bodies have not as yet floated ashore they would like to meet you." She rammed her hatpin firmly through the back of her boater. "You must be Luis, the sooner you introduce me to your brother and we get to work on that wound, the better. It is festering already."

Her violent attacker had metamorphosied into a round-eyed boy, he backed away into the shadows of the other room. Miss Daventry tutted impatiently and followed. Feeling as if I were in the middle of particularly bad and bizarre dream, I moved after them. His brother, fully conscious though breathing with difficulty, said weakly: "What, in God's name, is happening?"

It was, I thought, a sensible enough remark.

"This old ..." began the boy, but Miss Daventry interrupted him and introduced us both afresh. While she was talking she had taken off her hat and put it, together with her camera and binoculars, on the floor, and was now rolling the sleeves of her blouse up.

"Luis," Jose said. "Boil some water."

"Mother Mary," Luis said devoutly. "You are not going to take any notice of her, are you? The woman is a maniac, and a foreign maniac at that, she. ..."

"Do as I say," his voice was rasping. Briefly Luis hesitated, then, full of misgivings he picked up a large metal pan and limped away with it. Jose leant back, exhausted, against the white-washed wall.

His black hair curled thickly over his head, and under straight brows were fine eyes, golden-brown, that despite his weariness were still bright and keen, vivid under the black lashes. I could understand Carmen's anxiety for him.

Miss Daventry began to remove the blood stained bandage from his shoulder. "All the medical things are wrapped in a towel on top of the basket, could you be getting them ready for me, Alison? The sooner we see to these bullet wounds the better."

14

I did as she asked, and then dropped down onto my knees beside her. She had removed the make-shift bandage and the wound lay ugly and exposed. I tightened my stomach muscles as she scrubbed her hands vigorously, then, her sleeves rolled up, she turned towards Jose. I averted my head, staring out through the window, unshuttered now to give her as much light as possible. Bees hummed, darting in and out of the shade and I stared with undue concentration on scarlet begonias that massed the window bottom. There was a quick intake of breath and Miss Daventry said reassuringly: "There, that's done. You have been lucky. The bullet simply ploughed through the flesh, another inch to the right and it would have shattered the bone."

Silently I passed improvised swabs across to her as she cleaned the gaping wound and then bound it with bandage. No-one spoke. Luis watched every movement of Miss Daventry's deft fingers, and said, subdued: "Thank you ... we are ... I am sorry. You will accept my apologies?"

"On one condition," Miss Daventry said briskly, turning towards him. "And that is that you behave yourself while I see to you."

He nodded, paling visibly as she began to tear the trouser away from his leg and I saw that what I had thought was rust was congealed blood. A faint tinge heightened his cheeks and he clenched his hands into fists as Miss Daventry probed for the embedded bullet. Beads of sweat rolled down his forehead and then he gave a gasp as Miss Daventry triumphantly withdrew the bullet. He closed his eyes as she finished cleaning the ripped flesh, bandaging it firmly. Miss Daventry leant back on her heels, saying briskly: "Now all you need is some food, and we have plenty of that."

I began to unpack a large loaf of bread and thick wedges of cheese and one of Maria's tarts.

"When do we leave?" Jose asked as Miss Daventry passed him a bottle of wine.

My heart sank. It was a question I had been dreading. It seemed impossible that either of them would be able to keep the rendezvous with the boat.

"*A boat!*" Jose rasped, wiping his mouth with the back of his hand. "Are they all fools? After last night a boat will stand no chance!"

"It belongs to a German tourist and is crewed by Germans." I said, sounding more hopeful than I felt. "You and Luis will be hidden in case of a search. . . ."

"In *case* of a search," he stared at me as if I were mad. "There is no doubt of a search . . . and do you know how much room there is to hide on a small boat? None. None at all. The whole thing is suicide!"

"Father Calzada says it is suicide to remain here."

He swore angrily. Even Miss Daventry seemed deflated. I wondered wryly what the prison sentence was for helping Basque terrorists . . . and how on earth I had got myself into such a mess.

Chapter Four

As dusk fell we helped Luis out to the car. Jose seemed much fitter, his shoulder not giving him any trouble, but there was a dark sticky patch beginning to ooze through Luis's trouser leg and his face was pale.

The road curved down the mountainside and through a scattering of villages to the coast. All that could be seen in the darkness was the white flecked foam of the sea pounding against the cliffs. We rounded a corner and looked down upon the bay, sheltered between a sharp headland on the west and a ridge of cliff to the east, the wide sweep of sand, golden and inviting by day, was now nothing but a black, blank void. The wind was coming in flying gusts, whipping the Atlantic into white horses that plunged and reared up the distant shingle.

"Take the car as near the sea as possible," Jose said.

I could hear Luis's sharp intake of breath as I swung the car off the road and onto the rough turf, jolting inch by inch closer and closer to the luminous line of pale foam that showed where the sea ended and the sand began. The wheels began to sink and clog and I stopped.

"It's no use. If I go any further out I'll never get the car back."

"Come on," Jose said to me brusquely. "Let's walk down to the tide line and see if we can see anything from there."

Jose was breathing heavily and I wondered if his shoulder was giving much pain, and how he would manage to swim out to the boat with the sea running so high. We felt our way along the shingle traversing the full curve of the bay till we reached the barrier of the headland. Here the sea beat noisily, creaming against the smoothness of the rocks, deep and inhospitable. He drew me to a halt. "Can you hear anything?"

I shook my head. Gripping my arm once more he set off back, this time towards the eastern arm of the bay. For a few brief minutes the moon sailed from behind the banks of cloud and we could see the sand, firm and pale. This time we walked faster, and in ten minutes had reached the ridge of cliff that jutted out starkly into the ocean. The breeze was growing stronger and there was the spit of rain in the air. Nervously I waited as he stood, straining his senses for any sound or sight of the promised boat.

The sea drummed and surged, filling up the dark air around us, the white horses growing higher and wilder.

"If the boat does come," I whispered. "You won't be able to swim out in this."

"Ssssh," he said angrily. "Listen!"

Faintly I heard another noise. A humming and then, suddenly, I saw a pinprick of light flash on and then off.

"There!" he said sharply. "That's it."

Tugging me behind him he began to run across the sand, towards the black shape of the car. Luis was already struggling to stand, leaning heavily against the bonnet. Then we saw it, shrouded in deep darkness, laying low in the water, rocking and plunging just inside the arms of the bay.

"That's it!" Luis's voice was exultant. "They've come!"

"But they are not coming any nearer." Jose said grimly.

I felt my throat tighten as he dropped his jacket to the ground and kicked off his shoes.

"My dear boy!" Miss Daventry said, the wind tugging at her straw hat, blowing wisps of hair across her face. "Surely you can't swim so far out in a sea like this? Not with an injured shoulder!"

"There is no choice. The boat is waiting for us and it is not coming any nearer to the shore. If anything should happen before I get back, do not wait for me, take Luis immediately back to the cottage, understand?"

"Yes, but ..." she broke off in alarm. "Alison! What on earth are you doing?"

"I'm going with Jose. As you said, he can't swim out alone in a sea like this."

Jose did not hear me, he was already sprinting down to the sea. Heedless of Miss Daventry's protests I raced after him, my dress and sandals lying scattered at her feet. He was already waist deep, and then, as the icy cold of the water numbed my feet and legs, he disappeared amongst the waves, his arm rising ghostlike in the darkness as he struck out towards the boat. The silky water submerged me and then I was swimming steadily after him, shaking my hair out of my eyes as I tried to keep him in sight. The wind was blowing in strong gusts now and the waves grew higher, a holacaust of tumbling water, the foam crashing over my head drowning me for whole seconds at a time. Jose's voice sounded thinly over the roar of the sea.

"What the hell. . . ."

I swam up to him. "I'm all right." I yelled. "Keep going!"

He blasphemed viciously and then turned, heading once more straight out to sea. Another five minutes and I was beginning to wonder if my rash impulse had been justified. If Jose were in difficulty I had no strength left to do anything about it. He was treading water now, staring into the night.

"Where the devil has it gone to?" he gasped.

Breathlessly I swam beside him, all around us the sea swelled and heaved and far back in the distance I could see the faint silver line where the waves were crashing on the shore. It looked far, far away. . . .

We were too low in the water to see clearly. If they would only flash their lights again, anything to give us an indication of which way we should go . . . but the inky blackness that enveloped us remained impenetrable.

The solid mass of the rock stacks showed where the curve of the bay ended and the open ocean began. We were now parallel with them and the roar of the sea filled the night air, loud in my ears, drowning all other sounds. . . .

Jose shouted. "The boat was inside the arms of the bay. We must have passed it."

I blinked the foam from my eyes, nodding in agreement, deeply thankful that he had no intention of swimming any further out into the vastness of the indifferent sea. Hanging there in the black water I was experiencing fear, real fear, for the first time. I wondered which way the currents were running, if they would be against us as we swam back. . . . I pushed the thought away from me, struggling to remain calm. . . .

Jose took a deep breath and plunged away to the east. I swam after him, wondering if he had seen the boat, if it was near.

Suddenly there came a new sound, the distant throb of an engine. Jose was treading water now, gasping for breath. As I joined him I could see the black shadow of the boat low in the water, bobbing silently at anchor not twenty yards away from us, and I could hear the engines coming nearer.

The sea boiled around us, a raging mass of surging water, tossing us backwards and forwards, sucking us down into its limitless depths. Another wave crashed over my head, beating the breath from my body as I struggled for air. Then I saw it and hope failed.

Around the headland came the powerful hum of a speedboat, its searchlight sweeping the glittering, living surface of the sea. It was bearing straight towards the waiting boat and in another few moments, the cruel shaft of light would catch us in its glare. Jose dived away, heading directly back to the beach. My heart beating painfully I put my head down and followed. The vibration of the engines surrounded us, drawing nearer and nearer. Then there was sudden silence as the motor cut and all that could be heard was the suck and slap of water against wood and metal. The line of foam on the shore was luminous and distant, the black expanse in between colossal. Summoning up all my reserves of energy I fought to keep abreast with Jose. He was treading water again, shaking the spray from his eyes. Behind us the small boat was clearly visible as the police shone lights on her deck and began to board her.

"Come on," Jose gasped painfully. "They'll be searching the water next."

Once more we turned our faces towards land, swimming with

fresh urgency. The wind caught the voices from the boat, carrying the abrupt questions and the gutteral replies of the Germans. This time I could feel the rush and force of the water lifting me onwards, bearing me towards the shore, the relief I felt as I allowed myself to go with it vanished as the searchlight skimmed our heads and the motors revved once more.

They were right behind us, it was impossible that they should miss us. I wondered vainly which was preferable. Death by drowning or death by shooting. ... The wash from the boat slapped over my head, swamping me in black water. The prow cleaved the sea, veering to the left, the blinding light sweeping the coastline. The black silhouette of two figures were pinned down in the glaring circle of light that pierced the darkness of the shore. Helplessly I cried out as the boat, its light blinding its intended victims, skimmed the sea, closing in.

I heard Jose shout and then saw, between the foam and the flying clouds of spray, the two helpless figures turn and run. ... Terror engulfed me as I heard a shout of command from the speedboat and heard the rifle crack whistling shorewards.

"Bastards!" Jose was gasping. "The bastards!" Then he dived away to the right, swimming towards the rocks. Other shouts followed but I could no longer see, fearfully I swam in Jose's wake, my strength failing rapidly, the sea pulling insistently on my legs, weighing me down, sucking me under.

The cliffs stood out against the white gleam of breaking waves, then my eyes were blinded, the spray flying in my face. I could sense the nearness of the rocks but could not see them. Helplessly I floundered, swallowing water, coughing and spluttering as I struggled for air. Desperately I clawed out, reaching for a handhold, a foothold. ... The next wave lifted me high and I gripped slippery rock, hauling myself painfully from the surging depths.

Jose was still struggling in the roaring water and I leant forward trying to grasp his arm. Our hands met, then he was swept from my hold, submerged in the mass of foam and spray. Sobbing, I saw his head disappear and then nothing but the waves crashing against the rocks in a mass of white surf.

"Jose! Jose!"

The pale white of his face bobbed through the swirling water, one arm reaching outwards. I leaned forward, slipping on the treacherous rocks, stretching my arm out to his. Gasping and panting I dragged him up beside me, then, shivering and sick, strained my eyes to see what was happening on the beach. The speedboat was rocking at anchor a short way from the shore, the enormous lights stabbing down onto the pale sand. Dark figures were running up onto the turf towards the road. Of Luis and Miss Daventry there was no sign.

"We can't stay here." Jose gasped harshly. His face was contorted with pain and the soaking bandages were dark with blood. He began to feel his way along the rocks and I clambered after him, each yard an agony of suspense. The distant figures on the beach were fanning out now, combing the beach, approaching the cliffs.

"We'll walk straight into them!" I whispered urgently.

He shook his head, saying savagely: "We can't stay here, one sweep of their lights and we're done for. We have to reach the headland where there is some cover."

"What cover?" I whispered back, but he didn't bother to answer me. I slithered down a slope of shingle and he whipped round, hissing: *"For God's sake, be quiet!"*

The shouts of the police were nearer now, their bobbing torches sweeping in smooth arcs, there were only minutes left before they reached the rocks. . . .

"It's no use," Jose panted. "Into the water."

He gripped my wrist, pulling me downwards, slipping into the water without a splash. The rocks loomed above us as we cowered against them, the waves creaming around our heads and shoulders as we clung to the slippery surface. Jose scooped up a handful of wet shingle rubbing it over his face and neck so that only his eyes showed white in the darkness. I followed suit, the menacing footsteps drawing nearer.

The stab of the torchlight shone down yards away from us and I gulped air, thrusting myself below water, sinking down beneath the waves, holding myself under as long as I could, forcing myself to stay beneath the surface of the sea. With bursting lungs I had to turn upwards, up through the deep water to the foam flecked surface and whatever awaited me there. . . .

He had his back to me, the dazzling light scoring the jagged cliffs. I took a strangled gasp of air and dived deeply, pushing myself away. . . .

The sea above me was transformed into a myriad of sparkling bubbles as the torchlight pierced down on the water, and I knew he was waiting for me. My ears drummed and my chest was bursting and then it was too late. I felt my flailing hand grasped and a massive shadow above pulled me relentlessly towards the surface. The splashing foam stung my eyes as I struggled, gasping and sobbing for air, trying to find a handhold for my free hand, to wrench myself away from him. The rock slipped beneath my grasp, grazing my hand, searing my arm as I was dragged like a twisting fish from the depths of the ocean. The light burst about me, the air filling my lungs and a voice said harshly: *"I've got you. Now I've got you!"*

Chapter Five

I lay slackly on the wet rocks, gulping great lungfuls of air as Jose cursed steadily under his breath. The night was dark again, the pinpricks of light receding.

"I. . . thought. . . you were the police." I gasped at last.

"God help us," he panted exasperatedly. "They've gone. Look."

I looked and saw men wading out to the rocking speedboat.

"Miss Daventry and Luis?" I asked, starting to tremble as the cold wind bit into my damp flesh and the horror of the situation became increasingly clearer.

"I don't know," he said flatly. "I didn't see them after that first rifle shot."

"What do we do now?" I asked, teeth chattering.

"We get back to the cottage and then we find out what has happened to Luis. As he spoke he grasped my wrist, and surprisingly gentle, hauled me to my feet. I stumbled against him and the warm, sticky blood clung to my chest.

"Your shoulder! It's bleeding!"

"Yes," he said, already picking his way over the pitted rocks. "It is. Now follow me." Silently we climbed over the slippery rocks towards the curve of the beach. The moon floated opaquely out from behind its curtain of cloud as we reached the firm sand and from there to the turf and the point where we had left the car the going was comparatively easy. The beach was churned by many footprints and the grass where the car had been parked was flattened and scored by tyre marks, the gorse bushes nearby trampled and torn from their roots.

Jose circled the tyre marks, then bent down, trying to follow them as they disappeared into the springy turf.

"Did they get away?" I asked fearfully.

He stood, clasping his shoulder, staring at the ground. "I don't know." he said at last. "The car was certainly driven off in a hurry, but it could have been the police."

"Or could it have been Miss Daventry . . ." I said, filled with desperate hope. "They could be at the cottage now . . . waiting for us."

He winced, holding his shoulder, and in the moonlight I could see that the wet bandage, black with blood. Abruptly he turned, striding towards the road with a terse, "Come on."

I ran after him, the grass making our progress silent. When we reached the empty road he crossed it, skirting the thin line of trees that separated it from the open fields, and then dropping stealthily among the vines. Beyond us in the darkness loomed the dim shapes of hills and woods, and somewhere, miles distant, were the mountains and the cottage. My heart was beating light and fast as I padded after him, my ears straining for the sound of cars on the nearby road, dreading once more to see the menacing beams of light in the still darkness. A small animal brushed past my feet, startling me into a cry. Jose's hand tightened painfully and I tried to remember that I was supposed to be helping *him*. Our roles seemed to have reversed themselves. I was feeling more and more like excess baggage and wondered how he would take the suggestion that I should return to Miguelou. But it was no good. If I did that I would be tormented by visions of him collapsing on the bare hillside and bleeding to death. An encumbrance I might be, but at least I was fit and would be able to help him when the going got rough. His strength was amazing. Despite the loss of blood and the pain he was in, he moved swiftly through the fields, making straight for the sides of the hill and the belt of pines. Soon we were in the inky depths of the trees and the wind dropped. Our rapid walking had whipped some warmth back into my body, but I still had only my underslip on and both of us were barefoot. The pine-needles dug into the soles of my feet, pricking and stinging.

25

Then we found a narrow pathway and gratefully exchanged the tortures of the pine-needles for that of soft, dry sand.

When the woods petered out the path continued, winding like a pale snake up into the hills. We trudged on, heedless of the physical discomfort, heedless of everything but the necessity of reaching the haven of the cottage once more. The path grew steeper and I toiled beside him, wanting to know how his shoulder felt, dreading to ask. His breathing was hoarse and raw and his footsteps hesitant and stumbling. His hand clasped mine, guiding me on, then he pitched forwards, tripping over a gnarled tree root. He looked indescribably weary as he struggled to his feet, saying brusquely: "Come on. It isn't far now."

"Your shoulder," I said. "Let me see. . . ."

He swung away from me. "The blood is drying."

In the pale moonlight it looked freshly damp and the fear I had been fighting flickered into life.

"Come on," he said again, his voice little more than a thick whisper. "We can't give up now."

"Jose. . . ." I put a hand out to him and he grasped it, pulling me along beside him.

The breeze soughed through the branches of the trees below us, ladening the air with the pungent scent of the pines. Exhausted, I limped on, my feet hurting, my body cold, mind numbed.

The way seemed endless, time after time, I slipped and fell so that my slip was torn and filthy, my hands and knees grazed and bleeding, Jose was staggering now, eyes half closed. The night sky was lightening, the first chinks of the dawn appearing in the east, when he paused, pointing unsteadily.

"There, do you see?"

Ghostlike in the first pale rays of the rising sun, the mountain soared, misty and nebulous. He stumbled on and I trailed after him . . . down into the valley . . . skirting a cottage with hens and geese waiting for their morning feed . . . then up into a forest of cork oaks, no longer seeing anything clearly, my whole strength and effort being in putting one foot in front of the other . . . in keeping upright.

26

The sun came through the trees in patches of pale gold, but gave little warmth. I found it impossible to stop shivering as my slip clung clammily to my body and in ice-cold misery I trudged on, walking across more fields on a sandy path, then deep in the heart of the woods again. The cattle were up in the hills and we could hear the faint sound of their bells as we floundered on, hands grasped together, heaving weighted legs over ditches and through scrub and tangled thickets.

Swaying exhaustedly, Jose pointed. A hundred yards away across the hillside, was the ribbon of track and beyond it, safe and inviolate, huddling beneath the sweep of the mountain, the cottage.

I sobbed with relief, weaving dizzily across the open countryside, my eyes fixed on the blue of the cottage door. Eternities later I leaned thankfully against the wall as Jose pushed open the door, then I pitched forward, the light wavering, the blackness pressing in on me. Jose crashed against the stout wooden table and I called weakly: "Miss Daventry, Miss Daventry. . . ."

There was no reply.

Chapter Six

The echoing emptiness of the cottage seemed the final mockery. If Luis and Miss Daventry had been arrested by the police, then not only Jose's future looked black, mine did too. With difficulty I pushed the thought of Spanish jails to the back of my mind and wearily concentrated on making hot coffee. Jose was silent, immersed in thought, the bandages on his shoulder still wet with the dark stain of blood seeping through.

We drank the reviving coffee and then I braced myself for the task of removing the sodden dressing and re-bandaging his shoulder.

"Don't be nervous," Jose said comfortingly. "It doesn't hurt."

"I'm not nervous," I said. If he could lie, so could I.

For a minute I thought he was smiling, then I pulled the last swab away and he sucked his breath in sharply. It looked raw and open and my stomach muscles tightened as I washed the dried blood away, sponging gently till the wound was clean. He flinched once, staring determinedly out through the window as I gingerly re-bound it. At last I leaned back on my heels saying hopefully: "It looks as if it is healing. How does it feel?"

"Bloody awful."

"Yes, I suppose it does," I said unhelpfully. "What do we do now?"

"We can't do anything till we have some rest."

There was only one bed in the cottage. Jose heaved himself up from the table, reading my thoughts. "The bed is big enough for two. Perhaps you will feel better if you put some of Maria's clothes on."

I nodded, knowing what a fright I looked, my underslip muddy and torn, my bare feet black and bleeding. Wearily I searched through Maria's clothes till I found a scarlet dress, that apart from being two sizes too big, was wearable. Jose had dragged himself into the other room and fallen onto the bed. Tired beyond belief, I washed myself as best I could and then tied a scarf round my waist to gather the dress in. It wasn't what the best dressed woman of the year was wearing but it would have to do. Hesitantly I walked into the bedroom. Jose was already asleep and he had been right, the bed *was* big enough for both of us. I gazed round the spartan room, there was nowhere else comfortable enough to sleep.

Cautiously I slipped into bed beside him. He stirred restlessly, flinging one arm across me. There was nothing I could do about it and I was too tired to care. His thick dark hair brushed my cheek and I closed my eyes, sinking down gratefully into a deep, dreamless sleep.

I awoke to the golden light of late afternoon, my body stiff and aching. There was no sign of Jose and no sound of movement in the rest of the cottage. Groggily I swung my legs off the bed, filled with sudden horror.

How could I have gone to sleep when, for all I knew Miss Daventry had been arrested by the police, or even shot and killed? Hastily I ran into the other room, searching for Jose. From the remains on the table he had eaten, and the coffee in the jug was fresh and hot. The sun streamed through the open doorway, the soft breeze blowing in the fallen petals from the flowers on the window ledges.

I stood there, scanning the hillside for any sign of him. Five minutes, I thought. Five minutes. If he isn't here by then, I'm going to start walking to Miguelou. Perhaps that was where Miss Daventry was now, safe and sound, sunning herself in the garden at the rear of the inn. I refused to contemplate any other possibilities. It was probable that Luis had been arrested, but if he had Miss Daventry would have talked her way out of the situation. She should have said he was a hitch-hiker she had given a lift to. Anything, just as long as it kept the police happy, after all, governments don't like arresting tourists, it's bad for trade. I should have gone back to

Miguelou last night, not tramped over the hills, barefoot and cold with Jose. I wasn't wanted by the police. There was no reason why I couldn't return to Miguelou.

Thus reassured I went back into the cottage and poured myself a cup of coffee. When I had finished it I was going to begin the long walk to Miguelou, it did not matter if Jose came back or not. I had done my best to help and it wasn't my fault that I had failed. I had just about convinced myself when Jose's shadow fell across the floor.

The clothes he had on had belonged to one of Maria's sons. Maria's son had not been six foot tall and toughly built with broad shoulders and strong arms and he looked faintly ridiculous as he said tersely: "We're leaving."

"I had already decided on that. I'm going back to Miguelou."

I don't know what I expected. Thank you would have gone down all right. In the last twenty-four hours I had nearly suffered death by drowning and death by exhaustion. At least that is what it felt like. And all because of him. He didn't say thank you. He said:

"Like hell you will."

I stared at him stonily and put my cup down. "I'm going. Right now."

My exit was spoiled because he was still in the doorway and there was no way around him. He didn't move, just stood there, amber eyes holding mine.

"Please let me pass. I have to find out what happened last night to Miss Daventry and I can't find out by staying here."

"Agreed. And you won't find out in a prison cell either."

"I have no intention of ending up in one."

"Then listen for five minutes. What happened last night wasn't an accident or coincidence. Someone told the police where and when the boat was picking us up. And that someone will have told them that two Englishwomen were helping us, *and* given your names."

For a minute I believed him and my heart began to beat painfully.

"You can't know that!"

He shrugged. "You will soon find out whether I am right or not, but I wouldn't take the chance. The minimum you would get for helping a known member of ETA would be five years. For a member of ETA who had tried to smuggle weapons into the province, ten to fifteen at a guess."

I swallowed. "All the more reason why I should find out what has happened to Miss Daventry."

"I agree. That is one of the reasons I am going to Lindaraja."

He might just as well have said Timbuctoo. I said with barely concealed patience. "You can't go anywhere yet. After last night the roadblocks will be up again and they will be searching the countryside twice as hard."

"Lindaraja isn't a place. It's a hacienda. The police will have already searched it thoroughly and no doubt will have put a road block at its entrance. But we are not going in at the entrance. We are going in at the back door."

"We're not going anywhere. You can go where you like by yourself. I don't believe a word you say, you're just trying to frighten me. I am going to Miguelou. Now. This very minute."

"No you are not, Alison."

It was the first time he had used my name and it threw me off balance. I stared at him suspiciously.

"If you return to Miguelou the police will question you."

"I'm not sure that they will," I said with more confidence than I felt. "And if they did I wouldn't tell them where you are."

"Don't be a fool," he said exasperatedly, standing in front of me, blocking my exit to the door.

I said furiously. "A fool. How *dare* you say that! If I hadn't been such a fool you're wretched shoulder would be gangrenous by now *and* you would be hungry *and* thirsty. You nearly drowned me and nearly killed me with exhaustion. Do you think I like tramping over half of Spain in the middle of the night and with no shoes and hardly any clothes? I *could* have gone straight to Miguelou and slept in my bed all night. But I didn't. I stayed with you, and now you have the *nerve* to call me a fool. Well this is where I stop. From now on you can fend for yourself. I couldn't care *less* what you do. *And*," I said as a parting shot, looking pointedly at the too short trousers. "You look utterly ridiculous!"

The amber eyes gleamed dangerously and as he reached out for me I ducked down, hitting him with all my force across the shins. He staggered back against the wall, struggling to regain his balance, I dived beneath his outstretched arm, shooting out of the door into the sunlight, running over the slippery grass my heart hammering wildly. I sprinted across the track and into the thick cover of the trees, slipping and sliding into the bushy scrub, jumping precariously over gnarled tree roots and giant fungi. There was no sound of pounding feet following me and when I was safely deep in the pines I threw my arm around the rough bark of a tree, gasping painful breaths of air, grateful for the dappled shade. I was so intent on listening for sounds from the direction of the cottage that I heard the other sounds too late.

A chaffinch twittered and darted from a nearby tree and there was the sound of a branch being thrust to one side and the rustling of leaves as someone unseen moved through the trees and bushes towards me. There was no time to think. I swerved off in the other direction, twigs and saplings scratching my legs and pulling at my hair. A breeze ruffled the tops of the trees above me as I weaved between the pines, the ground shelving steeply.

It was so steep that when I saw him I could not stop. It was too late to turn and flee. My own momentum hurled me down a bank of earth and stones, falling and slithering amidst a cascade of leaves, hurtling directly into the arms of a rifle slung policeman.

Chapter Seven

He grasped me round the wrist, shouting for help as I fought like a madwoman. With all my strength I wrestled against the iron arms that now held me. I managed to get one hand free, twisting round to claw at his face . . . to get at his eyes, but it was too late. He moved his head out of my reach and then other hands gripped hold of me, and there was no hope of escape. It was the third time in twenty-four hours that I had been viciously manhandled and I was beginning to become something of an expert at inflicting damage myself. My nails ripped at his flesh, tearing the skin from the back of his hand as they pulled me away from him, twisting my arms behind me.

His shouts had brought more men and I was surrounded by black shiny boots and perspiring faces.

"Well done, Martinez," an exultant officer said, gazing at me, his hands on his hips. "Villada will be no trouble now."

"*What the hell do you think you are doing?*" I shouted as they began to climb the bank down which I had fallen, dragging me along in their midst.

"You'll soon see!" the officer said looking pleased with himself. "Martinez, you keep tight hold of her. . . . Amiano and Arias cover from behind. Fidel, you come with me."

Fidel, a thick moustache covering his top lip, grinned. "Why does Martinez get all the best jobs?"

"Because he's not as lecherous as you . . . we can't spend all day searching the woods for you and any skirt that comes along." He pushed the sweating Fidel in front of him. "Come on, another two hours and we'll be back in Bilbao . . . who knows, after this afternoon you might make officer yourself."

"Fat chance," Amiano said in an undertone from behind me. "If there's any glory to be won he will be keeping it to himself."

"Let go of me!" I demanded again. "This is ridiculous. . . ."

I was cut short as Martinez gave my arm an extra twist and I cried out in pain. There was no chance to bluff it out, to play the innocent tourist. The officer said gloatingly. "What a nice surprise for your boy-friend."

"I don't know what you mean," I said angrily. "Let me go at once, you're making a mistake. . . ."

He laughed, stroking his chin with his thumb. "You are the one who makes a mistake, a very big mistake."

They were dragging me between the trees, towards the open hillside and the cottage, their hands resting menacingly on the guns at their hips.

"*Let me go!*" I demanded again, my voice hoarse with fear. But it was no use and I knew it. The trees were thinning, the hot rays of the sun striking in brilliant shafts through the leaves. The last low lying branch was pushed to one side and the cottage lay in full view, cupped in its hollow, small and lonely beneath the massive purple sweep of the mountain. The men fell silent, gazing at it speculatively.

"Is he armed?" the officer demanded at last.

"No," I said. "And he is hurt. There is no need for those." I nodded my head in the direction of the guns. He grinned down at me, saying to Martinez, "It's going to be easy. Keep tight hold of her and keep her quiet."

My arm was pulled another painful degree higher and then they began to move stealthily out into the open. I knew what they were going to do, and I knew that I was powerless to stop them. I tried to think clearly, to free myself from fears grasp. I stumbled over a tussock of grass and Martinez swore, jerking me upright.

The cottage was only yards away now, its blue painted shutters shining in the sun, quiet and still, to all appearances bereft of life. A tiny surge of hope flickered through me. Perhaps Jose, rushing out of the cottage in pursuit of me, had seen the police, perhaps that was why he had not chased me, perhaps now he was safely hidden, watching from a distance. Amiano and Arias dropped flat down amongst the grass, their guns raised and pointing steadily.

"Jose Villada!" the officer called out, his voice ringing over the desolate hillside. "You are surrounded. Come out slowly with your hands raised."

I saw the imperceptible tightening of the fingers on the triggers: "*They're going to shoot!*" I yelled, before Martinez slapped his hand across my mouth, his nails clawing into my cheek.

"*You God-damned bitch!*" he said furiously, twisting his other hand through my hair, tugging my head backwards. "*You God-damned stupid bitch!*"

I was choking, pain knifing through me as he and Fidel dragged me nearer to the cottage till we halted, flanked by Amiano and Arias, half hidden by the waving grass, their fingers unflinching on the triggers.

"*Don't come out, Jose!*" I shouted frantically. "*Don't come out!*"

This time Martinez made no attempt to silence me, and the officer leaned his back against the mossy bole of the pear tree, a hint of a smile about his thin lips. "We know you are in there, Villada. There is no escape this time. Come out with your hands high!"

There was no reply. I strained my ears to hear any sound from the cottage but there was none.

"He's not there," I said with sudden hope. "He saw you coming and you are wasting your time. *He's not there!*"

The officer raised an eyebrow lazily. "Really? You must think we are very stupid." He nodded to Martinez and his grip tightened. As if he had all the time in the world the officer eased himself away from the tree trunk and wandered casually over to us. Then, still casually, he slipped his gun from his holster and pointed it at my head.

I am not the stuff heroines are made of, or martyrs. I licked my lips, clenching my hands into clammy knots, hanging on to the last edge of sanity.

"Villada," he called out pleasantly. "If you do not come out within the next three minutes, your girlfriend will die."

I heard, faintly, the whisper of wings as a bird settled on the crimson roof, and the slight rustle of leaves as the breeze sighed through the pear tree, but there was no sound from within the cottage.

"You are making a mistake." I said again, my voice little more than a croak. "I am *not* Jose Villada's girl-friend. He couldn't care *less* whether you shoot me or not!"

The officer considered this for a second and then smiled indulgently. "I think not," he said, and then shouted: "Two minutes left, Villada!"

Choking sobs were rising in my throat, chasing the last shreds of reason away. It seemed too preposterous, too unbelievable. I was on the verge of losing my life because of a man I had only known twenty-four hours and who was engaged to another girl!

"Please listen," I said, my breath coming in harsh gasps. "He isn't armed ... there is no need to shoot. . ."

Right on cue something flashed past my shoulder with a sharp crack and in the same instant Fidel cried out, grasping his arm where the blood spilt, oozing through his fingers, trickling down in giant droplets onto the grass. For a brief second the wooden shutter had opened, the barrel of his gun gleaming before he had slammed them shut again, bullets whistling into the splintering wood.

The officer's face was mottled with rage as he said viciously: "You will be sorry for that, Villada. Sixty seconds and then I shoot her!"

He began counting and I remember thinking that no-one would understand. Not ever.

"Forty-one ... forty-two ..." the officer continued.

A butterfly with jewelled wings fluttered delicately out of the shade, dancing gossamer light towards me.

"Forty-five... forty-six. . . ."

The cottage door moved slightly. I blinked my eyes, terrified that I might have been wrong. It swung wide and Jose stepped out into the burning sunlight.

"Let the girl go," he said tersely, dark eyes glittering. "She is a tourist, she isn't involved at all." He was unarmed, his hands high above his head. For a long, long moment no-one moved, and then the officer moved the barrel of the gun away from my head, swinging it in a graceful arc till it pointed at Jose, his index finger tightening on the trigger.

With a strength I didn't know I possessed I wrenched my hand free, swinging savagely at his legs, bringing him crashing to the ground, unbalancing Martinez, the report of his gun rended the air, whistling wildly over Jose's head before it fell from his grasp, thudding into the long grass within my reach. I dived for it, scooping it up in both hands, pointing it straight at him as he sprang to his feet, eyes blazing with rage.

"Tell them not to come near me or I'll shoot you!" I sobbed, terrified out of my life as Martinez made a move towards me. He halted tensely, ready to pounce.

"*Not yet* . . ." the officer hissed between his teeth.

Slowly I backed away, edging inch by inch to the open door, my eyes never leaving his, the gun in my hand never wavering, pointing lethally at his chest. He swore harshly, his empty hands clenching and unclenching, livid with rage as I backed away, Amiano and Arias watchful, their hands on their guns, waiting only for a word. I saw him lick his lips, tortured by indecision.

"I mean it," I said. "The slightest move from any of them. . . ." I stepped into the shadow of the cottage, my skirt brushing against Jose.

"*Get inside*," he said, as I backed into him. "*Now!*"

A bullet smashed into the stone inches above my head as Jose sent me stumbling into the dark of the cottage, slamming the door behind him. I dropped the gun, clattering, to the floor.

"It's no time to get cold feet," he said cheerfully, ramming another magazine into his gun. "Those bastards aren't going to take us carefully to Bilbao for a nice little trial. They are going to shoot. Shot trying to evade arrest, or English tourist accidentally shot in riot, take your pick."

A hail of bullets smashed through the wood shutters and Jose flung the gun I had dropped back into my hands. "For God's sake use it! If they think there's only one of us shooting they'll try to rush us."

"I can't," I said wildly, kneeling beside him beneath the window. "God, I can't shoot at police!"

"Why not?" he asked reasonably. "They're shooting at you."

I didn't answer. There wasn't time. A huge stone shattered the top half of the shutter, crashing down onto the floor, chips of stone flying like hailstones, followed immediately by the whine of a bullet singing over my head. Sheer terror made my finger curl round the cold metal and squeeze once, twice, the gun kicking back powerfully, jarring my arm and shoulder, knocking me backwards.

"You'll do better if you open your eyes."

"Go to hell," I said. And meant it.

"And that gun only holds nine bullets. You've spent two." He sent a magazine skittering across the floor. "And don't shoot like that. Hold your wrist with your other hand and keep your arms straight, point the gun at the target and *then* pull the trigger, and follow through with a natural pull up. That way the kick-back won't be as hard, and you have more chance of the bullet finding its target."

"*I don't want it to find a target!*"

"And don't jump ten feet in the air when the cartridges eject, they're supposed to . . ." he broke off, springing to his feet, eyes blazing. "*For Christ's sake, the door,*" he shouted as he leapt past me. "*The door!*"

He flung himself against it as it crashed open and in that blinding, agonising second, I caught a glimpse of black boots and a bullet ploughed into the stone floored room, ricocheting wildly, before the force of Jose's body slammed the door shut and he leaned heavily against it, panting, sweat pouring down his face.

"Well done," he said as I stood trembling, staring with fascinated horror at the smoking gun in my hand. "Did you get him?"

"No."

"Better luck next time." Jose said, kneeling beneath the window, levelling his gun once more. He stiffened, then gave a whoop of exhileration, spinning round to me.

"Can you see? Bloody hell, bloody, bloody *hell*!"

I caught a glimpse of a running figure on the periphery of the woods and then another, stouter figure firing from the shelter of a tree, before it turned, diving deep into the pines. I stared at Jose bewildered. "Who are they? What. . . ."

"It's Javier and Pedro!" he said exultantly. "*Look!*"

Amiano and Arias were racing across the hillside in pursuit.

"That only leaves three," Jose said lightly. "And two of them are injured."

"One of them," I corrected.

"Two. You shot the officer in the foot."

I felt the blood drain from my face and then he was putting a finger to his lips. "Keep shooting from the window," he whispered. "And don't stop till I tell you. The officer has disappeared, he must be round the back, probably nursing his foot. I'm going to try and get him through the rear window. Just keep the attention focused on the front of the cottage, there's a good girl."

"*No!*" I hissed back. "I can't, I. . . ."

"You don't have to aim, just keep his attention. There's only one of them out front. The other one is leaning against the tree uninterested in anything but his wounded arm."

"Which one is firing at us?"

"The fat one. The one that had hold of you."

"Good," I said and closed my eyes and fired.

Jose stepped cautiously into the other room, gun in his hand.

Seconds later there was the sound of struggling and swearing and I swung the gun round frantically, only a hair's breadth from shooting Jose. His gun was pressed in the back of the flushed and raging officer.

"It wasn't easy encouraging him back through the window, even with this, he keeps complaining about his foot."

I stared horrified at the blood seeping out of his boot.

"Keep shooting. His men haven't even missed him yet!"

The officer let out a stream of oaths, spittle forming at the corner of his mouth as Jose pushed him down onto a wood chair, beginning to lash his wrists behind his back. He blasphemed viciously, his eyes pinpricks of hate and rage.

"One down, two to go," Jose said with grim satisfaction. "Do you think we should put him in front of the window as target practice for his men?"

"*You'll die for this, Villada!*" he said, spitting in Jose's face.

"No manners," Jose said pleasantly. "And a bad loser. Let's see if the other two are any improvement."

"You out there," he called. "Drop your guns and come in here. If one shot is fired, the girl will blow your officer's brains out. If you do as you are told you won't be harmed. Just a little inconvenienced."

There was no reply.

"You tell them," Jose ordered curtly. "Or she will shoot."

If the officer had spared me the briefest of glances he would have realised that it was a bluff and that I was no more capable of shooting him through the head than flying to the moon. But he didn't. He glowered venemously at Jose and then said loudly. "Do as the pig asks. That's an order."

The pig smiled with satisfaction, and while I kept the gun at the officer's head, he strode to the door. Tight lipped, the injured Fidel and the furious Martinez stepped unwillingly into the room. With my gun still pointed at their officer's head, they allowed Jose to tie them to the wooden chairs.

"Beautiful," Jose said, his eyes dancing with pleasure as he pulled the rope tight. "Almost a complete set! And just to show there is no ill feeling, we'll even bandage you up."

"Go to hell," Fidel said, cradling his still bleeding arm.

Jose shook his head in mock sorrow. "You never know when to say thank you, do you?"

They didn't. Instead they swore with great energy and enlarged my Spanish vocabulary of obscenities threefold.

Jose laughed. "See to his arm, Alison. The lady of the house won't thank us if we leave blood stains all over her kitchen floor."

Thankfully I put the gun on the table and did as he asked.

Neither wounds were so bad. One bullet had ploughed its way through the flesh of an upper arm and passed out the other side, and I simply cleaned it as best I could and bound it with some of the bandages we had brought to the cottage for use on Luis and Jose.

The foot wound was the worst. Not because it looked serious, but because it was me who had inflicted it. He screamed as I tried to ease his boot off, calling me names I had never heard of before. I avoided his eyes as I sponged it clean, not daring to probe for the bullet, but staunching the flow of blood and praying he would get medical help before very long.

"*Whore!*" he spat at me as I rose shakily to my feet. "English scum. . . ."

Jose raised an eyebrow. "What did I tell you? They've got less breeding than they have brains."

"*You'll be garotted for this, Villada,*" the officer said through clenched teeth. "Salvador Ancioth took twelve minutes to die, if I have my way it will take you twice as long!"

"Charming," Jose said lightly, staring intently out of the window towards the distant pines. "Only one minor flaw. I haven't killed a policeman yet. Though no doubt it's a technicality that can be overcome."

There came the sound of rasped breathing and heavy footsteps thudded on the grass and then scraped to a halt outside the door, I drew my own breath in harshly, the icy touch of fear prickling my spine, staring round-eyed as the door swung inwards and Amiano and Arias surged into the room. A lump rose in my throat, threatening to choke me. I grasped at the table for support, my whole body trembling.

This was it. The end. All the future held for me was the inside of a Spanish jail, and then Javier pushed his way in behind them, his face distorted by a stocking mask, a gun held at their backs. His face split in a wide, triumphant smile.

"Is this a private party, or can anybody join?" he asked gaily.

Chapter Eight

I leant weakly against the wall as Jose tied and bound Amiano and Arias with enjoyable vigour. Pedro winked through his hideous disguise, slapping the palms of his hands against his paunch.

"Not a bad days work, eh?" he asked, his voice muffled.

"You're joking," I said bitterly. "It's been the worst day of my entire life . . . and it's still not over."

He said with a shrug . . . "It has been a little difficult, but soon you will be safe in France."

"France!" I said unbelievingly. "You're as mad as he is!"

Pedro exchanged glances with Jose and grinned.

"France is the only destination for you now."

Jose straightened up, ignoring the foul language from his prisoners, and said: "Let's know the worst."

"The worst is that there are warrants out for your arrest."

Jose's face was grim. "What the devil happened?"

Pedro's voice darkened. "It was Garmendia," he said heavily. "He is insane. He deliberately wrecked our plans to smuggle the arms in. . . ."

Jose's voice was barely controlled. He said tightly. "Garmendia betrayed us?"

Pedro nodded, and beneath his mask Javier's distorted features blazed with savage anger. "Jaime's death is on his hands," he said passionately. "And all the others who died. It was all Angel's fault . . ."

Jose's face had whitened. "Was it?" he said softly. "Was it, indeed."

Pedro said in a low voice. "He thought you were too soft, Jose. With you out of the way he thought he could control the local

42

ETA units himself . . . and he has. They all believe the attempt to smuggle in arms failed because of you, and that it was your fault so many men died. Angel is behaving like a madman. He and Alphonso Cia murdered Motrico's mayor . . . and it was Angel who tipped off the coastguards about the rescue attempt last night, and gave Alison's name to the police. He wants you dead and out of the way, Jose. And if the police don't do it for him, he will do it himself." Pedro cleared his throat uncomfortably. "There is even worse."

No-one moved and the silence lengthened tensely. He said at last, not looking at me. "Both you and Alison are wanted on charges of murder."

"But that's ridiculous!" I cried out, the room reeling around me. *"They can't! It's not true!"*

Jose caught hold of me, his arm tightly round my shoulders.

"Like I said," Pedro continued. "Garmendia is a man possessed. His own brother died that night on the beach because of his treachery. The last twenty-four hours have been a continuous chain of bombs and shooting. Early this morning it was Motrico's mayor. Later a bomb exploded in the town hall at Zarauz. No-one was injured but it was a miracle. And he has support. All the lunatic fringe are behind him. As we left to come here and warn you, they were rioting in Amorebieta and the police were rounding up demonstrators . . . all hell is breaking loose. And according to the latest news bulletin, you and Alison killed a coastguard in the early hours of this morning whilst escaping arrest."

"We didn't," Jose said curtly. "And I'd like to know how that son of a bitch framed us!"

"It would have been easy," Pedro said with outspread hands.

"Garmendia knew what time you were to be picked up by the boat. He tipped off the coastguards, and if you did escape then he was nearby. He fired the shot that killed one of them and you and Alison are left to take the blame."

Jose said hoarsely, "I'll kill him. God help me but I'll kill him."

"Not this side of the Pyrenees you won't." Javier said practically.

"One sight of you and the police will have you in Carabanchel, if you live that long."

"None of you will live that long!" the officer sneered triumphantly. "Not one of you will set foot on French soil . . ." he broke off abruptly as Javier jabbed his back with the butt of his gun.

"You're in no position to threaten anybody. I would keep quiet if I were you . . . unless you want a posthumous award."

The officer's eyes burned with anger and an ugly red stain flushed his face and neck, but he clamped his mouth tight shut staring venemously at Javier as he turned his back to him.

He and Jose moved towards the door, heads close together, whispering so that the listening policemen could not hear. Pedro sighed, saying softly so that I could hardly catch the words. "Jose came back from Argentina last summer. Since then he has re-organised all the local ETA units, before, they were a shambles, and psychopaths like Cia and Garmendia were killing and bombing under the cloak of Basque nationalism. Jose put an end to it. He negotiated with Madrid from our headquarters in Bayonne, with a coherant plan for Basque autonomy and he was beginning to have success. Angel saw his chance of discrediting him and took it, even though his brother was killed in the process, now nothing will stop him. The whole Basque region is going to be plunged into bloodshed again." He patted my shoulder comfortingly. "But another twenty-four hours and you will be with your friend, miles away from here and for you, this will be nothing but a bad memory."

"My friend!" I jerked my head upright. "But you never said. . . . Where is she? Is she hurt? What happened?"

"She is waiting for you in Bayonne. With Luis. She telephoned the inn at six this morning."

Relief swamped me. Ridiculously I wanted to cry. "But *how?* In heaven's name, *how* did she get Luis across the border?"

The warm, friendly eyes smiled. "That is a mystery. But I am not surprised. Not knowing Miss Daventry. She is a very enterprising lady."

"She is indeed," I said fervently. "I only wish I was with her."

"And miss all this excitement?" Javier asked, turning towards me, his eyes alight.

"It's not excitement. It's a bloody nightmare," I said crudely, and saw Jose give a flicker of a smile.

"What are you going to do with our private collection?" Javier asked him, nodding towards the smouldering men.

"A day without food or water will do them no harm, and by then we will have sailed safely to Bayonne."

"No matter how deep on French soil you go, I will hunt you down, Villada." The officer spat at him. "The French government doesn't want to upset Madrid. And the French police are our allies."

"But the French Basques are not," Jose said, picking up his gun and thrusting it into his holster. "And France has a law of political refuge that will shelter us. Be grateful for the fact that we haven't killed you."

"You're going to pay, Villada," he hissed, shaking with fury. "You scum! You bloody Basque bastard, you. . . ."

"Javier," Jose said, ignoring the flow of obscenities. "It is time to go, they won't wait for us long. The tide will change in another hour."

The officer glowered, spitting at us as we filed out of the room, his bitter voice still cursing us as we stood in the shade of the pear tree, the shadows lengthening around us as the blood-red sun sank behind the mountain.

"Will you be able to make it?" Pedro asked Jose anxiously. "It is a hard climb and Alison is already exhausted."

"Make what?" I asked, filled with fresh alarm.

"To Lindaraja," Jose said off-handedly. "I told you before. It is our only chance."

"But I thought we were going by boat, you said someone was waiting for us."

"Let's hope the idiots in there are just as gullible," he said dryly, nodding his head in the direction of the cottage. "Pedro and Javier are returning to Miguelou to track down Garmendia. We are going in the other direction. Upwards," he pointed to the mountain. I licked dry lips, saying hoarsely: "Isn't it possible to go round? Why is it necessary to climb the summit?"

"There is no way round without running into road-blocks. At Lindaraja we can pick up horses and equipment. Our only chance is to cross into France across country. We need to start now, before the rest of the light fails, I'm banking on the fact that the exact whereabouts of our friends wasn't known. If it was we stand no chance. If it wasn't, then we have perhaps a day in hand."

Javier handed him a torch and flask. "Good luck," he said, and turning to me grinned. "Perhaps a night out in Bayonne, eh?"

"If I ever live to see it," I said bitterly.

Jose had already turned and was striding out, leaving a trail of trampled marguerites behind him, Pedro gave me a comforting pat on the back, and facing the inevitable, I turned to follow. As I did so Javier pulled the stocking mask away, his dark curls rumpled like a small boys. He moved forward and kissed me on the cheek. "Good luck, and may the Saints go with you," he said.

With my eyes suspiciously bright I turned my back on him and followed Jose up the dust blown track.

Chapter Nine

The twilight was deepening rapidly, the mountain crests dark and menacing against the last lingering rays of the sun. We rounded the dark mass of the rhododendrons, the pine-needles rustling beneath our feet as we picked our way carefully to the lake.

The luminous surface of the water glittered silk-black as we skirted its banks, my shoes sliding on the dampness of fallen leaves and slippery moss. Minutes later we were in the open. The first faint stars glimmering in the darkened sweep of the sky as we stood on the narrow path that girdled the mountains flank. From the bottomless depths on my right hand side the wind came in flurrying gusts and I halted, my heart beating painfully.

He turned round, eyebrows raised questioningly. I cringed back against the comfort of the trees as far from the blind abyss as I could possibly get. I said haltingly: "I can't do it. I'm sorry, Jose. But I can't walk out there in the darkness ... the drop is sheer ..."

With surprising gentleness he grasped my hand, labouring with his injured arm to hold the torch.

"Let me," I said hesitantly, taking it from him. I shone it downwards, a brilliant shaft of light, on the treacherous path. The pine-woods on our left soughed and danced beneath the growing wind, the sheer drop on our right pulling me dizzily towards it as stronger and stronger headwinds pulled at my hair, my dress, tugging me towards the lip of crumbling stone. Inch by inch we edged our way painfully along, Jose's hand never leaving mine, urging me persistantly onwards, keeping me away from the pull of the cliff, away from danger. ...

It was an eternity of dark and fear and harsh breathing before the path led inwards, losing itself beneath the thick trunks of the pines and groves of impenetrable bushes. The blackness was thick now, pressing out everything but the beam of bright light from the torch, as we plunged into the depths of the trees, stumbling over gnarled roots, finding a way round the matted thickets, and all the time we were climbing steadily higher, pushing aside damp and fluttering leaves, the wind roaring now, tossing the branches of the trees, whipping my hair across my face as I pushed away clawing brambles, striving to find a clear passage through the maze of fallen boulders and the web of clinging vines.

The trees began to thin and as I raised the torch higher, all I could see ahead in the arrow of dazzling light was rocky ground, perilous with inky-black gullies and high above, the fierce, forbidding buttresses of the mountain rising crest after crest.

Jose's pace never slackened, with laboured breathing we scrambled over great boulders and slithered over avalanches of loose stone.

Then at last, despairingly, I felt Jose's great weight no longer supporting me and leading me on, but leaning heavily against me, his breath coming in harsh rasps. As we skirted a fall of rock he stumbled, swearing viciously. I held him, the sweat soaking my body, exhaustion engulfing me. He sank to the ground and I crouched beside him, unscrewing the flask of spirits that Javier had given him. He drank deeply, pushing the flask back into my hand. I took one mouthful then another, the strong spirit burning my throat, warming my tired body. I leaned back, eyes closed, drawing on whatever reserves of strength remained. When I opened them Jose was already struggling to his feet, the dressing on his shoulder moist and gleaming. I stretched out a hand tentatively and he turned away.

"Your shoulder . . ." I began, but he thrust the flask back into his pocket.

"We've nearly done it," he said, his voice hoarse with fatigue. "One last push. Come on."

I thrust my body beneath his good arm, and the nightmare journey began again. The shale beneath our feet slipped and slid like a live thing till we were on hands and knees, literally clawing our way upwards.

The moon had risen, pale and luminous, lighting the way before us. The mountains peak rose in sharp silhouette, an indomitable barrier between us and safety. Exhaustedly we clambered upwards, circling the gullies that sliced the rock asunder, inching our way step by careful step, in constant terror that the ground beneath our feet would give way, would topple us down the stark walls of rock, smashing into the pitiless scree.

I wiped the perspiration from my face, struggling for breath, amazed at Jose's strength, terrified that at any moment it would fail, with shaking hand I pointed the torch up and above me. The summit was there, a bare sheet of naked rock, glittering sleekly beneath the yellow ray of light. The wind whistled about our ears as we stood high and exposed, half-senseless with fatigue. With one last superhuman effort we moved upwards again, scrabbling for handholds where no handholds were, slithering backwards whole feet at a time, clutching desperately at any crevice, any ledge, any fissure that we could haul ourselves up by. My hands were numb, my mind a blank. Just one more step forwards, one more leverage upwards . . . I could feel hysteria rising in my throat as I clung and scraped and dug my way towards the summit.

Then the ground shelved, the wind tore at us in deadly gusts, but nothing rose ahead. No inky-black wall of rock, no dreadful buttresses, no unclimbable slabs of sheer stone. With a sob I sank to my knees, Jose's arm around my shoulders as he gasped painfully: "We made it! Thank God, we made it!"

The wind tore the words away from him, flinging them to the elements as we clung together like children, my frozen body wracked by sobs. Then, from the great high vaulted summit we edged our way downwards, grappling for footholds, clutching at any finger hold possible, till with hands grasped we staggered onto turf and moss and the ground beneath our feet no longer slid in cascades of loose earth and flurries of pebbles, but was firm and solid and safe. The dark malevolence of the peak was behind us now, below were trees and shadowy leaves and the carpets of pine-needles and narrow tracks made by unseen animals. Wearily we stumbled into the depth of the woods, resting every few yards against the bole of a tree, the branches shrouding us with shelter, the pine-needles comfortingly soft beneath our feet. Even the wind had dropped, whispering down through the leaves, fanning our burning faces.

Suddenly his grip on my hand tightened, his body taut, straining his ears for another, foreign sound. Faintly I heard it too, the distant whinny of a horse being carried on the night wind. My muscles tightened in panic but Jose's face was exultant.

"It's Roque! He's come to meet us!"

"Are you sure?" I gasped anxiously. "What if it's the police?"

He shook his head. "No. It's Roque. Javier said he'd try and get a message through and he has."

I didn't have the strength to ask who Roque was. I didn't care. By the tone of Jose's voice it meant friends and help and an end to the horror of the blackened mountainside.

Pressed close together, supporting him as much as my exhausted body could, his heart hammering against mine, we began to inch forward one painful step at a time. Through the cover of the trees a silent figure emerged, breaking into a run as he saw us. I was vaguely aware of his exclamations of shock and thankfulness and then, bruised and weary beyond all endurance I fell to the ground and would have stayed there uncaringly if the stranger had not said gently:

"Please. Can you help me get him into the saddle?"

I swayed to my feet, exerting every ounce of strength left to help Jose. He sagged in the saddle semi-conscious, his arm hanging lifelessly, the bandages sodden with blood.

Roque mounted another horse and hoisted me up behind him. Like a rag-doll I clung blindly, my arms around his waist, hanging on precariously as we descended the mountainside, the horses picking their way slowly and carefully. Bumping and swaying I closed my eyes, succumbing to utter weariness.

It was only the sound of other voices and the bright flare of burning torches that aroused me. Dazedly I stared around me as unknown hands lifted me from the horse and strong arms carried me across a splendid courtyard. A fountain of sparkling water rained down in a delicate mist and then we were in a large hallway where glittering chandeliers dazzled my eyes, shining down onto a floor of gleaming marble. Wonderingly I looked around me as I was gently lowered into a velvet covered chair, a kaleidoscope of colour surrounding me. Silk lined walls of glowing flame, rugs of honey-pale saffron, glowing shadows flickering across dark paintings in heavy guilded frames. Vaguely surprised that delirium was so sweet I closed my eyes, drifting off into sleep.

I dreamt that I was being carried up a sweeping flight of stairs, past high arched windows of stained glass, the glimmering light shining on panes of vermilion and emerald and topaz. That gentle hands were removing my shoes, that the soft burr of women's voices crooned above my head as my body sank into a soft bed and I was covered with crisp sheets. Then the fever eased and I slipped into deep sleep, dreaming intermittently of Jose and Miss Daventry and with somewhere, just beyond my grasp, a sickening sensation of fear and dread.

Chapter Ten

I lay back against the soft pillows, gazing uncomprehendingly at the slatted shutters through which the sunlight fell in broad golden bars. I turned my head, searching for familiarity. My room at the inn had been plain and austere. The only colour the coral-red of the wild roses that Carmen gathered daily, brilliant and defiant against the simple walls of stark white. Here, the walls were covered with a tracery of delicate carving in rich dark wood. Gorgeous wall hangings hung luxuriously, the dancing arrows of sunlight bathing them a soft gold. The bed I lay in was huge and grandiose, a four poster with fragile lace canopy and silk sashed drapes. Above me gilded angels and cherubs frolicked and danced and through the half open shutters I glimpsed a tiny balcony crammed with pots of scarlet geraniums and troughs of sweet-smelling bouganvillea.

I swung my feet off the bed and ran to the window. Below me the morning light shone brilliantly down onto a courtyard surrounded by walls of pale ochre. Tendrils of hanging creepers with star shaped leaves trailed the sun-baked walls and wisteria blossom hung in violet blue clusters, clinging to the swirls and loops of wrought iron window balconies, cascading over shaded archways. Through them I glimpsed horses and the shine of bridles and polished harnesses.

A fountain spouted a stream of water from the open mouth of a bronzed fish, the sun glistening through the fine spray, misting the myriad droplets into a thousand sparkling diadems.

I turned, searching for Maria's dress and sandals. There was no sign of them. Instead, a freshly pressed blouse and cotton skirt lay across the foot of the bed, and neatly below them stood a pair of soft leather shoes. I dressed quickly, stepping out into the high ceilinged passageway beyond. The floor was a mosaic of tiles, cool and smooth. I wandered past the windows, jewelled with stained glass, set deep in embrasures of solid stone, until I came to the magnificent staircase of my dream. I ran down the sweep of shallow steps and through the colonnaded hall into the pattern of sun and shadow.

As I stood there confused and hesitant, a man strode from the direction of the stables. On seeing me he paused fractionally beneath the archway and then smiled, strolling across to me, his arms held wide in a welcoming embrace.

"Good morning. I hope you feel better after your sleep?"

"Yes thank you ... but who. ..."

"I am Romero. Jose's brother."

He had the same devastating good looks, but there was something softer about the eyes, something less sensual about the mouth. He was dressed casually in riding breeches and high, gleaming black leather boots. A friendly smile creased the lines of his face.

"You must be hungry," he said, taking my arm. "Come with me. Breakfast is prepared for you, an *English* breakfast, would you believe. I've ordered Jose to stay in bed, but how long he stays there is anyone's guess."

He led the way through dim corridors and sudden patches of light as the sun's rays spilt through an open window. Then into a room lined with shimmering sienna silk, seating me at the head of a polished mahogany table that would have seated sixteen. A flushed young girl, her hair curling damply round her cheeks from the heat of the kitchen, brought in crisp rolls still warm from the oven, and a plate of bacon and eggs and gently fried tomatoes. The French windows were thrown open, the air sweet with the tang of lemon trees and wisteria.

Romero seated himself at my side, pouring out dark, strong coffee, handing me salt and pepper and a fine linen serviette.

"Despite the unfortunate circumstances, Alison. Welcome to Lindaraja."

"Thank you," I said, and then, trying not to sound rude. "When do I leave?"

He smiled. "Soon, unfortunately. Lindaraja has already been searched by the police, but there is no telling when they will come again." He leaned his head against the back of the ebony carved chair. "When you have finished perhaps you would like to see Jose. He has been asking for you."

I drank my coffee, grateful for its warmth. We had undergone two journeys of ordeal together. The flight from the beach and the climb to Lindaraja. The third and last journey, the most dangerous, the escape into France, was still to come. It wasn't a comforting thought.

When I had finished, Romero led me once again up the graceful curve of stairs and into the shadowed corridor. Through the open windows doves cooed soothingly and I could hear the gentle spray of water from the fountain. Romero paused before a door of intricately carved wood, hinged and studded with bronze. His hand gripped the heavy handle and pushed. Surprisingly, I found I was suddenly nervous and shy as I walked in behind him.

Chapter Eleven

He was sat up in a giant four poster bed, clean and freshly shaved. His hair still a knot of tangled curls and his amber eyes bright and refreshed, alight with good humour.

"I see you made it in one piece."

"Only just," I said dryly.

His hand reached for mine, gripping it hard for a brief second, then he said to Romero: "Any news of Garmendia?"

Romero shook his head. "No, but it's not surprising. The Bishop of Bilbao himself has been threatened with arrest, and a state of emergency has been declared for the whole province. The authorities have admitted that one hundred and ninety-eight people have been arrested in the last forty-eight hours. Six priests have been arrested. One of them Father Calzada."

Jose's eyes darkened. "There is a lot to be done and not much time to do it in."

"Don't worry," Romero said as Jose made to get out of bed. "Rest. You'll need it. I'll see to everything."

Jose's eyes met mine again for a brief tantalising second, and then I followed Romero out of the room.

He said: "It would be a good idea if you got acquainted with the horse you will be riding. You *do* ride, don't you?"

"Yes, but I've never attempted anything like this before.

He smiled. "Solitaire is a good horse and Roque will look after you."

With sinking heart I wandered out into the radiance of the courtyard, shielding my eyes from the brilliance of the sun's glare, letting my fingers trail among the cool, feathery-green fronds of the plants that clung around the fountain, the spray falling over my face and shoulders in a cooling mist.

Roque's shadow fell across the white stone and I looked up, noticing with something of a shock that he was not as young as I had at first thought. Tall and aesthetically thin, still dressed in riding clothes, he said almost shyly, "Romero would like me to introduce you to the horse you are to ride tonight."

I followed him beneath the brief dimness of the archway and into the noise and bustle and smell of the stables. The horses leaned sleek heads over their stalls, pale manes against chestnut and copper. A young boy with rosy cheeks led a glistening chestnut horse towards us.

"Solitaire," Roque said, slipping the saddle into place. The horse raised its head to mine and it was love at first sight. He was heaven to ride, and out on the gentle slopes of the mountain, the air blowing fresh from the summit, I forgot my worries and for a short time was joyously happy. Roque broke in on my happiness.

"You are a good horsewoman. You will manage."

He helped me down from the saddle, slipping Solitaire's bridle off and leading him to a box of hay. With a last look at Solitaire, nose deep, foraging for the food, I made my way back into the house.

Jose was waiting for me. Dressed and hands on hips he stood in the marbled hallway. I stopped only yards away from him, our eyes locking.

"Well, well," he said appraisingly. "Quite the accomplished horsewoman."

"I never said I couldn't ride."

His eyebrows raised expressively above gleaming eyes. "They say some people are born to it."

"And?"

"You are," he said, with a slight nod of the head, the tight black curls rippling. "I can tell."

We stared at each other, still not moving, eyes never wavering. Then the laughter in the amber eyes died, the flecks of gold like motes in a sunbeam, intensified, desired. With one swift stride he was against me, by body pinned firmly to his, his heart hammering wildly against mine, as the dark head bent and demanding lips met my own.

From a far distance came the singing of a lark, and my arms were still round him, pulling him to me with the same fierce intensity in which he was holding me. It was a long, long kiss, and when at last he raised his head he still held me imprisoned in the circle of his arms, and I still stayed, a willing prisoner, seeking no release.

"Well," he said, the blaze of desire hot in his eyes, still holding me transfixed. "Who would have thought it?"

I could feel his heart thudding against my own, my own desire flaring like the sudden upsurge of joy that had been mine with Solitaire out on the wild mountainside.

"Not me," I said, my breath hurting like that of someone who has run a long, long way. Someone who, in only seconds has travelled inumerable light years. "Not me," and I lifted my mouth to his again, my lips bruised and crushed beneath the pressure of his.

It was Romero who disturbed us. How long he had been there I didn't know. At the same moment we became aware of his presence and turned, still locked together, to face Romero's questioning eyes. Slowly Jose released me.

"You have mapped the route?" he asked.

"Yes, but we need to go over it together carefully. Very, very carefully. Even then it is only going to work if the God's are on our side."

Jose's eyes met mine. "They're on our side," he said, and I blushed and turned, leaving them with their maps and notes, slipping light-headedly along to my room.

The blinding light of the sun struck hotly through the windows and I closed the shutters, standing in the dimness, my blouse clinging to my body like a second skin, wet and clammy with sweat. I peeled it off, stretching my arms high above my head, seeing my darkened reflection in the mirror against the wall. I dropped the blouse onto the bed, padding into the adjoining bathroom. Slowly

I turned the taps, dropping my skirt and underclothes to the floor, the smell, the taste of Jose, lingering around me.

Then I froze, staring blindly at the gushing water, my whole body ice-cold.

"Oh God," I whispered weakly, fumbling for the taps, halting the rush of water, staring unseeingly down into the quivering depths. Then I stumbled back into the bedroom and sat down heavily on the bed. In front of me, specks of dust fluttered in the bars of slanting light that seeped through the closed shutters. The doves were back, cooing and fluttering. The faint whinny of a horse was carried lightly in the still air. The joy and perfection, the exultant happiness had been knifed, murdered to death by someone I had not given a thought to over the last twenty-four hours. Someone I had forgotten entirely. Who could take away from me all the brightness and brilliance that I had believed to be mine. There was, quite simply, Jose's fiance. There was Carmen. It was Carmen he loved. Carmen he was going to marry.

My head ached as I tried to think clearly. I stared unseeingly at my naked reflection in the shadowed mirror. What was it Miss Daventry had said on that first, fateful morning? I had asked her if any local men had been on board the boat trying to make for the safety of Miguelou's harbour and she had said: "Four. Among them Luis and Jose Villada. Jose is Carmen's fiance."

If the tears pricked my eyes before they fell I didn't feel them. Happiness had filled me, surrounding me like intoxicating music. For a brief fragment of time I had believed myself at the gates of paradise. Now the nectar and ambrosia, the musk and civet, had turned sour. I saw it for what it had been. For the past three days we had faced death together three times. His kiss had been the culmination, the natural reaction of a man with Jose's nature. It had been a kiss . . . only that. Not love. Simply a kiss, given lightly and no doubt expecting to be taken lightly.

Unless . . . hope flickered, struggling for life. Unless in these past three days he had fallen in love with me. Was prepared to relinquish Carmen? And if so, then surely he would tell me. Put his feelings into words. Leave me in no doubt of his love for me. And if he didn't? a small voice asked.

Then if he didn't, my joy was killed. I could see only a future without love, or at least the love I wanted. I sat bleakly, wondering how such a craving could be overcome, wondering how I should ever be able to get used to living without him.

Numbly I resumed filling up the bath. I lay there, the hot water doing little to comfort my turmoiled emotions but easing my aching body. There were more skirts and blouses hanging over a chair and as I slipped my arms into a freshly laundered blouse, I wondered cynically if they were, in fact, Carmen's.

Cries of greeting and hurrying feet reverberated through the rooms. I stopped, hand in mid-air, straining to catch the sound of the visitor's voice. If it was Carmen's. . . .

A door closed and silence fell. I ran quickly along the corridor and down the wide sweep of stairs. I had to be put out of my misery quickly. I had to know who the visitor was. I headed straight for the room from which muffled voices could be heard and with only a brief knock, and without waiting to be asked to enter, opened the door. My sigh of relief must have been audible. The visitor was Javier. His jeans were frayed and caked with dirt, his tee-shirt splitting wide at the shoulder, his plimsolls were scruffed and his hands and face looked as if they hadn't seen water for a week. He was the nicest, dearest sight in all the world. He flung his arms wide, swinging me round.

"You look wonderful! I shall hold you to your promise when we reach Bayonne. Think how those peasants will stare! The French think only they have beautiful women, but we shall show them, Alison. By all the saints we shall show them! We shall stroll down the Rue Marengo and drink pernod and they will admire you and envy me! And then we shall. . . ."

Jose tapped him on the shoulder. "Leave your arrangements for Bayonne until we reach Bayonne. What do you think of this?"

Javier shrugged, eloquently regretful, and turned to the map spread out on the scrolled carved table. My eyes sought Jose's, but he, too, had turned. I crushed my disappointment. I was being unreasonable. The flight into France was uppermost in Jose's mind. Surely that was natural enough.

The three dark heads pored over the rolled out map, fingers pointing, Romero tracing a faint pencil line, his brow furrowed in thought.

"That has to be it," Jose said at last. "And it has to be now."

"Now?" I asked, surprised into speech. "But I thought we were leaving it till nightfall?"

"The police are already on their way here. Javier was in Metebbe when he heard Lindaraja was to be searched again. With even more thoroughness. If he hadn't been so near to us we would have been caught like rats in a trap. As it is we only have minutes left."

As he was speaking he was rolling the map up, thrusting it down his broad leather belt, walking rapidly out into the hall and across the courtyard and into the stables, while the rest of us hurried after him. There was no time to feel alarm. Within seconds Roque had me in Solitaire's saddle and was mounting a nut-brown stallion with pale flowing mane and flaring nostrils. There was hardly time to say goodbye to Romero. With a firm handclasp the brothers parted, Jose swung easily up onto the back of a chestnut roan and with a whoop of joy Javier mounted a horse that was already pawing the ground with impatient hooves. The gates were flung open, and leaving Romero alone, surrounded by the rest of the horses whinnying with frustration in their stalls, we walked the horses carefully out and onto the smooth turf. Roque rode beside me, Javier was behind, and in front was Jose.

He turned, his eyes holding mine, saying with them what could not be said in words. I smiled back, my body filled with warmth and confidence. It was going to be all right. Everything was going to be all right.

I could see the tangle of curls growing thick in the nape of his neck, the firm, hard muscles, tense and ripple as he turned the horse's head to the left, picking a careful path between rocks and stones as the green of the lower slopes were left behind and we approached the rampart of pines and presumably safe cover from Lindaraja's unwelcome visitors.

I longed to touch him. To be touched. But now was not the time. Soon, when we were in Bayonne, when we could talk. ... On reaching the cool green shelter of the trees, Jose paused, swinging round in the saddle, his face stern, his eyes preoccupied. Far below us Lindaraja stood like an exotic toy of brilliant white. The hillside falling down green and lush, surrounding the glittering walls, plunging far below to where the snake of a road could be seen winding along the floor of the valley. The cars were easy to see. Tiny, gleaming dots of jet-black, they were sweeping at great speed along the length of the road, four, five of them. We backed the horses even deeper into the leafy dimness of the woods, leaning forward, hands resting on saddles, watching intently.

Beetle-like the cars curved through the valley, the road sweeping round in giant loops, bringing them steadily higher and higher. For a short while they were masked by trees, and then we saw them quite clearly, the steep leek-green meadows falling sharply on either side of the road. They wound upwards, towards the splendour of Lindaraja, and with bated breath I watched as the first car swerved to a stop in a cloud of pale dry dust at Lindaraja's massive gates. No-one spoke. In horrified fascination we stared at the drama being played out below us.

The cars were all there now, and dark figures were racing into the house and across the courtyard to the stables. It was difficult to see clearly as the sun was in our eyes, but I saw them seize the stable boy, saw him struck once, twice across the face. I forced my eyes away, desperately searching for Romero's familiar figure. The shouts of the men echoed and re-echoed, alien sounds amongst the peaceful serenity of the trees.

The shutters were slammed wide open, and two figures in skirts fled down the steps clinging in frightened hysteria to the bronze rim of the fountain, then running to the gates and the road beyond.

Only once did I steal a glance at Jose. And in the vicious set of the lips, in the knotted muscles of face and neck, the raging eyes, the white knuckles clenching into fists of iron, I saw his suffering and I could not look again.

Then, heart in my mouth, I saw Romero. He was struggling with a darkened figure at the top of the flight of steps that led to Lindaraja's pillared entrance, then in the next minute he was sent sprawling, rolling down the ochre steps by the kick of the man behind him. Mesmerised, like the eyes of a cornered animal, I stared as he staggered to his feet from the dry clouds of sandy dust, only to be pushed viciously in the back, sent reeling against the fountain, the myriad droplets of jewelled spray raining down on his head and neck. He leant double, gasping with pain, struggling for breath. The sun glared, and with shielded eyes I saw the rifle butt raised, gleaming unmistakably. I bit my knuckles deep, not daring to flicker so much as an eyelash. The menacing figure was too slow, with all the strength he possessed Romero knocked the rifle from his hands, heaving the man bodily over his shoulder, plunging him face down into the ripples of the playing water. His victory was brief, seconds later he was the centre of a mob and Jose drew his breath in sharply, digging his heels into his horse, wheeling him round, plunging back down the hillside towards Lindaraja, shouting: "For Christ's sake! It isn't the police! It's Garmendia and Cia!"

Chapter Twelve

It took Javier only a second to react, then he, too, was slapping the rump of his horse, disappearing amidst a clatter of stones and rustling leaves, charging down the mountainside after Jose, his horse's mane flying in the wind.

Seconds later, paintings, pottery, statuettes, anything they could lay their hands on came flying through Lindaraja's opened windows, crashing in ruins at Romero's feet as he knelt in the dust, forced there by the two men holding him, his arms held cruelly high. The treasures of generation after generation were smashed against walls, destruction for destruction's sake ran wild and I was glad that I could not see the anguish on Romero's face as he struggled helplessly, forced to witness the violation of his home.

"Oh my God," I whispered to Roque, in new, increasing terror. "Look!"

A grotesque figure, a blazing torch held high in his hand, raced across the courtyard, only inches from where Romero still struggled. Like some damned Olympic runner with the eternal flame he brandished it high, before plunging it obscenely into the heart of Lindaraja.

A faint flicker of gold licked tentatively round the edge of a smashed window, then spluttered into crimson life, sucking in oxygen, bursting out into a roar of flying flame. It licked voraciously along the window-frame, sparks flying like fire-flies, igniting the slashed velvet curtains of the next window, flaming into sheets of fire as it fed on the splintered contents of the room, blazing now from several windows, white-hot tongues scorching skywards.

Romero, still held, was dragged back to the high bronze gates as the heat seared their faces, as the interior of delicately carved wood and ornate draperies ignited like a tinder-box, sending huge soaring clouds of dense smoke billowing out over the valley, the stench of burning wood filling our nostrils as the breeze caught hold of the smoke carrying it up on a great upsurge of air.

Within minutes Lindaraja was ablaze, a flickering mass of gold and red, then men fleeing down the steps, their shouts of blind destruction now those of fear and panic. The flames flared higher and higher, and the smouldering, racking fumes thickened the air so that Romero was lost from sight.

Then, in the hideous flush that now filled the valley, we saw the dark silhouettes of Jose and Javier, sweeping down towards Lindaraja, forcing their horses nearer and nearer to the leaping flames.

I thought my head would burst with panic and horror of a magnitude I never dreamt existed. With a moan of pain that I hardly recognised as my own, I pulled on the reins, digging in my heels, and Solitaire swung round, neck low to avoid the overhanging branches, racing after Jose and Javier.

I heard Roque's cry clearly but took no heed of it. I had to be with him. Had to be there. Had to help, however ineffectually.

With a rattle of loose stones and pounding hooves Roque caught up with me, leaning over frantically to grasp Solitaire's reins, but I was having none of it.

"No," I shouted, the wind whipping my hair away from my face. "No!"

I turned my head to his, seeing the indecision in his eyes and shouted again. "It's no use, Roque. We have to help!"

His uncertainty fled, the solemn face was white and drawn. Without another word he let go of Solitaire's reins, racing down the mountainside towards Lindaraja, only yards behind me.

The ground was steep, littered with rocks and boulders, but Solitaire found his own way, galloping at full pelt while I strove to see Javier and Jose ahead of me.

Dust rose in swirling, choking clouds and then we were on turf and Solitaire thudded on, my ears filled with the sound of his pounding hooves, the very ground seeming to throb beneath the drumming onslaught. Roque was passing me now, the chestnut of his horse gleaming wet with sweat, thundering down the last slope to Lindaraja.

The entrance to the stables yawned open and I checked Solitaire's speeding gallop, steadying his head, gasping with fear as he reared away from the flying sparks, then obeyed, clattering into the stables and what looked to be hell on earth.

Great billows of smoke swept chokingly round me as I slid off Solitaire's back, sending him out through the gates and into the safety of the mountainside. The holocaust of leaping crimson tongues was veering towards the stables, the sparks igniting the wood above the horse's stalls, their hooves beating with terror in their trapped tombs. Through the flare I saw the runing figure of the stable boy, dodging bits of falling, blazing beams, racing across the heat of the courtyard flinging open the first of the stall doors as the fire took firm hold, crackling and leaping across the stable roofs. His arm was raised to protect his scorching face as he desperately slammed the bolt back, the horse rearing with terror before galloping out of the yard, mane flying in the wind, burning pinpricks of flame scattering its back.

"Let them out," Roque yelled to me as he and the stable boy wrestled with another horse too terrified to flee. "For God's sake, open the stalls!" I ran to the nearest stall, sparks showering down as I pulled the bolt free and the horse charged past me, knocking me to the ground. I caught a fleeting glimpse into the courtyard as I scrambled to my feet and I could see running figures, and a holocaust of fire consuming Lindaraja's heart, but I could not see Romero or Javier. Or Jose.

"The horses!" Roque shouted above the pandemonium. "There's two more . . . over there."

He was gasping for breath, his face blackened with smoke. "They'll need help . . . they're too terrified to leave by themselves. . . ."

The heat of the fire burned against our faces as we sped to the last stalls. The stable boy galloped past me, clinging to the neck of a horse, both his hair and the horse's mane alight with fire. The horses were rearing petrified, their hooves cleaving the air, as deadly as the fire that surrounded us.

"Keep back . . ." Roque yelled, struggling to blindfold the horse's eyes with his scarf. "Keep back. . . ."

And then both horses were free and Roque was pushing me after them, out into the centre of the stable-yard, down the narrow corridor between the flames. He moved in front of me, leading a black stallion struggling with fear and then with an almighty crash, a blazing log fell between us, linking up with the fire on either side, cutting me completely off, sealing me in.

"The main gate!" Roque's voice shrieked over the tumult. "Make for the main gate!"

I backed away from the wall of fire, head down, my arms across my face, staggering back through the ever decreasing alley way free from flames, making for the archway into the courtyard.

With stinging eyes I sought vainly for a passageway through the flames, but the belching smoke blinded and choked me and with every step I expected my clothes to catch light, to be consumed as surely as Lindaraja.

If I could only follow the wall round, keep my head down, my wits about me. . . . "Don't panic," I kept repeating to myself. "Don't panic, don't panic," and then in despair, "Jose. . . . Oh please, please . . . Jose. . . ."

The scorching hot walls were free from flame, the fountain a garish, fevered red in the glow from the burning house, but flying timber kept crashing down, creating hellish bonfires round which, somehow, I had to circle. And then it was too late. With the noise like that of an avalanche, the very centre of Lindaraja seemed to flare, seething upwards in monstrous flames, and a furnace of towering wood crashed down above my head, separating me from the fountain and the gates and safety.

Faintly I could hear Jose desperately shouting: "Alison . . . Alison . . ."

But there was no way through. I was circled by fire. Half senseless in the reeking fumes, my skin burning with pain as the leaping flames danced higher and higher, and the acrid smoke filled my mouth and lungs. I choked, cowering down, semi-conscious with fear.

Through the roar and crackle of devouring fire my terrified brain registered once more his frantic cries of: "*Alison! . . . Alison!*"

For a split second I saw him. Arm across his face, sparks flying in his hair, straining to reach me and it seemed to me that as I watched, the flames rose up around his feet consuming him totally.

Chapter Thirteen

I was retching, gasping for air, struggling back to consciousness.

"Oh God," he was saying thankfully. "Oh dear, dear God," and he knelt over me, the tears mingling with the black of the smoke, his arms protectively round me, his body trembling as much as mine. I took a heaving breath of air, my eyes stinging excrutiatingly, and turned my head in the safety of his arms.

The sky was a blushing vapour of red and orange, the whole mountainside bathed in the flush of the fire and I was far away from it, out on the barren heights and above me were the concerned, smoke-streaked faces of Javier and Romero. And the anguished face of Roque.

"There was nothing I could do . . . there was no way back. . . ."

He fell down on his knees, grasping my hand as I laid on the grass supported by Jose. I knew I was crying, but then so was everyone else.

I said weakly: "I know that Roque . . . I know."

He gripped my hand tight and then straightened up, patting one of the horses.

"Solitaire?" I asked weakly. "Solitaire?"

Against the incandescent hillside I could see him, a magnificent silhouette, the wind ruffling his mane. Romero, tears glistening on his cheeks, threw one arm around me, the other round his brother's shoulders. No-one spoke, silently we watched Lindaraja in its death throes, the air aflame with showers of sparks, the heat, even from a distance, palpable. The roof collapsed in a shuddering roar, one great last beacon of flame surging skywards, then the molten ruins began to subside and burn themselves out.

Jose said bitterly. "At least there is nothing left for the state to take from us," and with one last tortured look, he swung his horse's head round and we followed him deep into the heart of the darkening pines.

Faint and weary I patted Solitaire, finding some measure of comfort in his warmth and strength. The pines were interspersed with oak and ash, and the tossing leaves caught in my hair and brushed dryly against my cheeks as I bent low to avoid the overhanging branches. We were no longer climbing, but with Jose in the lead, were picking our way carefully along the mountains flank. The trees began to thin and without their shelter the wind tore across the uplands, tugging my hair across my eyes, striking chillily through my cotton blouse. Solitaire paused at times, picking his way carefully over the uneven ground, circling thorns and brambles, never putting a step wrong.

Roque was nearby, caring and protective, and now and then Jose would swing round, and though it was too dark for me to see his face, I knew he was smiling at me, giving me encouragement.

Out in the open the horses moved easily, cantering over the short turf, the rampart of tall swaying pines to the left, the scree and ravines above them, grim shadows beneath the milk-white of the moon, and to our right the hillside descending steeply, and somewhere, far below, was the road and the fleeing mob led by Garmendia and Cia.

Wisps of cloud drifted over the moon, plunging us into deeper darkness and I did not know whether to be grateful for it or not. With such a moon we would not easily be seen, but without it our way would be even more difficult.

We had reached, God alone knew how, a flat, grassy plain stretching ephemerally out on either side in the blackness. Jose's horse began to gallop, the hooves thundering in the stillness. Javier and Romero were flying behind him and I gripped tight with my knees and followed, Solitaire's mane of pale cream streaming in the wind, Roque hard behind me.

The land shelved, deepening down, and the horses gallop increased, until once more all there was in the world was the feel of Solitaire beneath me, the rush of wind tearing at my skirts and hair, and the supple muscles of Solitaire stretching out to the full. I could see Jose check his horse, veering to the right and heard Roque's shouted instructions. I did as he told me, swerving past the bank of plunging ground, too exhilerated to feel fear.

We flew through the open countryside, avoiding the dark cluster of hamlets and villages, and often seeing, from our welcome distance, the wraith-like snake of a road. Slowly we began to climb, the turf giving way to barren ground and rocks. Just as I was beginning to think my aching muscles would take no more, Jose reined in his horse and waited for us to reach him.

"They need a rest and a rub down," he said to Roque. "And we need to eat."

Roque tended the steaming horses and we sat in a tight circle on cold slabs of stone and uneven boulders, and Jose passed round bread and chunks of cheese and bottles of wine. Then he sat beside me, leaning his back against a smooth rock, one arm around my shoulder, drawing me close to him as we ate and drank in silence. Romero sat with hunched shoulders, his pain at the loss of Lindaraja evident in every movement. I was tired, my eyes heavy, longing for sleep. Only Javier retained good spirits. He grinned at me, pushing his thick hair away from his face.

"This is better than a night out in Zarauz, eh?"

"Is it?" I asked, eyes half closed, content to be beside Jose, to feel his body so near to mine, to be together. . . .

"Miss Daventry was in the International Brigade during the civil war," he said undaunted. "She would have enjoyed this. Some of the tales Pedro has told us about those days . . . do you know they were both in Guernica on the day it was bombed?" he whistled admiringly. "What a lady that one is. . . ."

Jose stirred, ruffling my hair with his hand. "The next hour is the crucial one. Javier knows the border like he does the streets of Miguelou. We should be in France before the dawn."

"And we should be on our way," Javier said, standing up. "We stand no chance once the sun rises."

Jose squeezed my shoulder, his lips brushing my hair as he helped me to my feet. "Frightened?" he asked.

"No," I said truthfully, my fingers interlocked with his. "Not when I am with you."

For a moment I was in the circle of his arms and he was laughing down at me, dark eyes gleaming.

"Good," he said, then helped me mount Solitaire. "It's nearly over now."

All thoughts of any danger we were in as we tried to cross the border illegally were far from my mind. I was still warmed by Jose's nearness. My heart and mind full of him. I longed for Bayonne and a chance to talk. A chance for him to tell me about Carmen. More than anything, I needed him to tell me about Carmen. I felt a slight flicker of fear, then determindly thrust it aside. I had seen the expression in his eyes when he looked at me. Seen love and desire there. Surely that was enough? 'Bayonne,' I whispered to myself as we began to move forwards again. "Please, *please* let us reach Bayonne. . . ."

The way was more difficult now. No lights from lonely cottages gleamed in the distance. The darkness was thick and total. Gingerly the horses picked their way, climbing higher and higher, stones and pebbles clattering in heavy falls as the horse's hooves disturbed them, seeking for secure ground. The isolation of the wilderness that pressed in on us became menacing and frightening. Giant in the darkness were the black density of mountains and forests. The higher we rode the stronger were the gusts of wind that swept across us and soon the gleaming black buttresses of rock were all around us and I could hear Romero swear beneath his breath as he struggled to guide his horse onto what little safe ground there was.

With growing apprehension I saw the first paling of the night sky in the east, and smelt the damp of the coming day. We were in single file now, the rock hemming us in on either side, squeezing through with only inches to spare. Suddenly Jose halted, the wind tearing at him, carrying his words away almost before we had heard them.

"If there is going to be trouble, it is going to be in the next fifteen minutes. From here it is downhill and straight into France. It's a route Javier has taken many times." He pointed away to the east. "The nearest road is in that direction, if there is any trouble it will come from there. Don't stop. Not for anything. Better one captured than all captured."

Spumes of cloud still masked the sky, but they were racing harder now and there was the damp spit of rain in the air. The path before us was narrow and tortuous, a sliver of space between the ink-black of the rocks. The sound of the horse's hooves rang metalically against stone, and then, as we emerged, the rolling hillsides of France stretched ghost-like in the grey of early morning, hill after hill, with the slender rim of the moon sinking down, tingeing the slopes mother-of-pearl.

For minutes, hardly daring to breathe, we reined in our horses and searched with aching eyes for the signs of army or police. Nothing stirred, only Solitaire's head moved as he stretched his neck, his mane cascading caressingly over my hand.

With a deep, purposeful intake of breath, Jose said softly: "Come on. This is it. And remember, don't stop. Not for anything."

With infinite care he rode out of the protective shadows of the rocks, guiding his horse slowly and quietly across the open ground, over the indefinable line that severed Spain from France. My heart palpitating painfully, I urged Solitaire to follow Romero and Javier, and Roque, as always, stayed in the rear.

Those few short moments, that brief spell of riding that took us across the frontier, seemed to hang timeless. The sight of the men in front of me, supple bodies on strong horses that were breaking into a loose canter, creamy tails swinging in the breeze, defiantly beautiful against the rose of the coming dawn, is etched in my memory forever.

I stroked Solitaire's gleaming neck and he flung his head up. Then he was off, cantering past Romero and hovering at Javier's side.

He turned his head, giving me that irresistible face splitting smile, his eyes exultant.

"It's been easy," he said joyfully. "Tonight we will be in Bayonne!"

The road was so far away, only an indentation amongst the grey-green landscape, that I didn't give it a thought. Like Javier, I felt relaxed and free and safe. So that when the shot rang out, my heart lurched into my mouth and I was numbed.

From the distant line of the road came the pinprick glint of motor cycle mirrors. Roque slapped Solitaire's hide, shouting frantic orders as the horses broke out into a break-neck gallop, their hooves pounding like thunder over the firm ground, whipping up clouds of dry pale dust. Jose swung round, wheeling in the dust as he galloped beside me, staying protectively at my side. In front was the gleam of Romero's horse and the fleeing hooves and Romero crouched low and tense, his dark hair merging into the mane of the galloping beast.

Javier was abreast with him, his horse plunging across the hillside, and then the second shot rang out and I remember thinking to myself: 'Fools, how can they hope to hit us at this distance and this speed,' and then the next thing I knew was Roque's scream and the dragging thud of his body as it fell from the saddle, foot still caught in the stirrup, and my own panic at not being able to curb Solitaire's wild flight and Jose's horse rearing round, high on his haunches, his nostrils flaring, his hooves deadly inches away from my face. And then I had slithered off Solitaire's back, running with pain in my heart and my head, racing back to where Roque lay lifeless in the dew spangled grass. There must have been other shots but if there were I was oblivious of them, and then Jose was thrusting me violently aside, kneeling over Roque's body, shouting at me to continue.

"*Is he all right? Is he dead? Oh God, is he dead?*" I cried frantically, trying to see Roque's face and Jose's arms pulled me aside, flinging my physically from the inert body.

"I told you to stop for nothing!" he yelled, his face contorted with rage and grief. "Get the hell out of here!"

I was stumbling to my feet, hands and knees sliding over slippery grass, my breath hurting so much that I could hardly gasp out yet again:

"But Roque! Is he dead? Is he?"

"*Yes!*" Jose shouted, spinning away from the body that had never moved since it had fallen so heavily to the earth. "Yes, he's dead. *Dead! Dead! Dead!*"

His fury filled my ears, reverberating through all my senses. I was blinded by tears as he hurled me on to Solitaire's back and with a slap on her hide sent me careering off after the distant, fleeing figures of Romero and Javier.

Chapter Fourteen

Solitaire charged over the turf, Romero and Javier a cloud of dust in the distance. Pounding hooves were behind me, and then Jose drew abreast, heading Solitaire downhill. I could see a huddle of houses and gasped breathlessly: "But the road. . . ."

Jose, white-faced and grim, shouted only: "Keep on."

"But. . . ."

"Keep on!"

The rain began to fall, fine arrows that sprayed my face, merging with the sweat that soaked me. The hillside sloped steeply down to tended fields, the stone and slate of a farmhouse growing clearer, the half dozen cottages straggling out in an uneven arc beyond. Far ahead of me I saw Romero and Javier wheel round, disappearing in the direction of the farm. Solitaire lunged after them and I was crying tears of grief and fear, hardly knowing where one ended and the other began.

A cart track led away from the farm, up to the hills where there was pasture for the cattle. Solitaire veered down it, Jose only feet behind me. Down between fields of sad looking wheat, the rain falling heavier, blinding my eyes and stinging my face. Ahead was the bleak farmyard and untidy outbuildings, and Romero and Javier's horses lathered and steaming, and then Solitaire plunged across the rutted yard, rearing up as a strange man shouted and reached for his head. I was hurled from Solitaire's back, hard on to the cobbles of the yard, terrified as the frightened horse struck the air above me with flashing hooves.

Jose slithered from his horse, scooping me up from the dust and dirt, racing with me into the farmhouse. The man ran behind us saying frenziedly:

"Quick. You must be quick!"

The room was large with a high raftered ceiling and flagged floor. A dog stirred near the massive fireplace, ears pricked as Jose swung me to my feet at the foot of a ladder that led up to the dimness of the rafters. Hardly able to regain my breath or my senses, I climbed urgently up in front of Jose. Strong arms reached down for me as Javier dragged me into the dark and then Jose was beside me, pulling the ladder in after him. Lowering the square of wood that sealed us in, leaning back against the wall, panting for breath.

"Dear God," he said fervently, and then in the dark his hands reached out for me, pulling me fiercely towards him, burrowing his head in my hair. We were crouched on the floor, Javier and Romero opposite us, gasping in lungfuls of stale air. As his breathing steadied, Jose said hoarsely to me. "The man is Javier's uncle. He was expecting us."

"Not like this, he wasn't!" Javier said.

"What will happen?" I asked, my heart hammering wildly. Jose leant his head back against the wall, his arm around my waist.

"Technically the Spanish police can't operate on French soil. But it sometimes happens. It all depends on the mood of the French police at the time. From the point where they saw us the road swings away, they wouldn't be able to see where we went, but as this is the first farm for miles they would be idiots not to guess we were here. Another ten minutes and we will know for sure."

I licked dry lips. "The horses," I whispered. "Whoever comes will see the horses."

"Too damn right they will," Romero said defeatedly, his head in his hands.

Javier slapped him on the back. "You think my uncle can't lie his way out of this. . . ."

"If he lies like you, then there's a faint chance," Romero said grudgingly.

Jose's hand tightened around me. There came the unmistakeable sound of a speeding car shooting into the farmyard, skidding to a halt.

"This is where we start to pray," Javier said softly.

Jose moved, lying full length on the sawdust floor, his eye to a glimmer of a crack in the floorboards. Nervously I stretched out beside him, straining my ears to hear what the raised voices at the open doorway were saying.

Javier's uncle, hands raised despairingly to heaven, shoulders shrugged high in helplessness, stepped into view. I had barely seen him on my frantic arrival at the farm. Now he stood only feet below me, the veins in his neck standing out, his face mottled with rage.

"My best horses!" he shouted, outraged. The shadow of the man he was talking to fell across the table, but he remained just beyond my range of vision. "They took my best horses! There was nothing I could do, they were armed." His voice rose sharply. "And now you ask *me* questions, and let those bastards get away. They can't be far. . . ."

"No," the other man cut in icily. "They can't be far." It was a voice I had heard before.

Javier's uncle spat in fury. "Your men are wasting their time, searching my farm. I've told you what happened. Those devils have taken my horses. . . . And what happens? After they rob me, you ransack the place and no-one wants to know. If I complain to the local police, what will they do? Nothing. Sweet bloody nothing!"

He slammed a huge fist onto a wood table and the dog moved up beside him, ears flat, growling softly. "No-one wants to know. And my animals will be gone for good!"

Javier was right. He could lie. I nearly believed him myself. He was a powerfully built Basque with a swarthy skin and fierce black eyes, his whole body consumed with rage as he slammed his fist once more on the table.

"Don't we have any rights at all? This is France . . . not Spain!"

"Shut up, fool," the other said contemptuously. Other footsteps rang across the yard and into the house.

"No sign of anyone," a third voice said, strangely familiar.

I strained to see them, but my line of vision was cut off at the table. If they would only step forward a foot. . . .

"Of course there is no sign of anyone," Javier's uncle said scornfully. "How many more times do I have to tell you. The lunatics you want are getting further away every minute you spend here!"

The other man drummed his knuckles on the table and I could see the sleeve of Spanish uniform.

"You search where you want. You are wasting time. *They are not here!*"

"But they came here, and only minutes ago. Strange that we did not see them as they left, don't you think so?" the voice was hard as steel.

"My God," Javier's uncle exploded. "I am a Frenchman, terrorised by your bloody separatists, not able to live in peace, not defended by my own police and victimised by Spanish police! I'm no ignorant peasant to be terrified of you. You have no legal right here. None. None at all."

He moved forward threateningly. The man he was speaking to never flinched. His shadow stayed unwavering.

"Careful, old man," he said.

A fourth pair of feet hurried into the room. A voice that belonged to Amiano said breathlessly. "They aren't in the outbuildings."

I could sense the officer scanning the room, studying the dim recesses of the rafters.

He said. "I can *smell* them here."

Javier's uncle lowered his voice, saying viciously. "I'll see to it that this outrage doesn't remain a secret. You have trespassed over the border once too often."

My nerves tightened as the other said softly. "You are lying. They are here, aren't they? I *know* they are here."

He stepped forward, directly beneath me, the bleak light of early morning full on his face. He looked as unpleasant as he had last time I had seen him.

"Martinez," he said, "I want those horses shot."

Jose's hand tightened on mine as the blood pounded in my ears.

"All of them?" Martinez asked.

"All of them. After all, they don't belong to this gentleman. He can't possibly have any objections."

"And what about the animals those terrorising bastards took! When do you get those back for me?"

"Shoot them, Martinez," the officer said again. I saw Martinez shrug and leave the room. My chest felt as if it were being squeezed by iron bands.

"You know who the men were who came here?" the officer asked.

"For the hundredth time, no. *No. No. No.* They were Basques and they were desperate *and* they were thieves. They didn't introduce themselves!"

"Two of the men were Villada's."

Javier's uncle shrugged. "So what?"

The officer laughed softly. "Come, even you must have heard of the Villada's."

"The name means money . . . not thieving terrorists."

"I've heard the Villada's have a passion for horses. They won't be too pleased with you when they see the rotting carcasses in your yard."

"Mother Mary! All I want is some justice. All the time you spend here talking, they are getting further and further away."

"Are they indeed? Let's see how far away they are when they hear their horses being shot. The sound will, I think, carry quite clearly into the loft above this room."

Jose tensed beside me and I bit on my fist, fighting back the rising tide of nausea. The sound jarred my eardrums, sending my nerves singing with fear. It was a lifetime before I realised that the sound had not been that of a gun, but of a car. Doors slammed shut and an impatient, authoritive voice spoke angrily in French.

"What is the meaning of this? Why are you and your men here?"

"We were chasing terrorists. Four men and a girl. They are wanted on charges of murder. We shot one of them near the frontier, the others, two of them Villada's and an English girl, came here on horseback. Those are their horses outside."

"And what crimes are the animals guilty of, that they are to be shot?" the French policeman asked sarcastically, walking across to the table, his men behind him. I heard Jose take a quick breath of surprise, and then the Spanish officer gave a strained laugh.

"None, comrade. We have searched the outbuildings thoroughly and have not found them. They are in the loft above this room. I was trying to trick them into showing themselves. Wait, and I will show you."

I closed my eyes and prayed.

"You will leave this farm immediately."

"But. . . ."

"*Immediately*. We have had instructions that we are not to co-operate any longer with your activities this side of the border. Ponistowski, the Minister of the Interior, has given his word that the French policy towards refugees will be that of shelter. In his own words. We shall be strict in dealing with violence but there will be no abuses. This, my friend, is an abuse."

The officer swore unbelievingly. "They are here," he yelled. "Not ten feet away!"

"For the last time I would be obliged if you and your men would return to the frontier."

"Look at this!" he shrieked, pointing down to his foot, heavily bandaged and on a rocker. "That whore with them did this, and you ask me to return to Spain without them! Never. Not while I draw breath. I swore I would see Villada dead, and I shall!"

"Maybe," the French officer said. "But not now. This man has told you what happened. They took his horses and went further into France."

The Spaniard was seething with frustration. "They are here I tell you! Two of the Villada brothers and an English girl. One minute. Only one minute and I will show you!"

"You will leave immediately. Your senior officer will not be very pleased if publicity is given to this . . . not so soon after the statement made by our Minister. Certainly not to pursue a personal vendetta. Allow me to escort you off the premises."

White with rage the Spaniard was surrounded by the French

police and forced to leave the room. The sound of their voices faded and I could no longer hear. Minutes later a car engine throbbed, and amidst shouted insults on both sides, the Spanish police left the farm. The French officer walked back into the house.

"Thank you," Javier's uncle said with heartfelt thanks. "They would not listen to me. . . ."

"How many horses did they take?"

"Four, they. . . ."

"You surprise me. I wouldn't have thought a farm this size had so many fit animals." He tapped his foot on the stone floor. "If I were you, I would take care of those horses outside. I know the Villada's. I went to school with Jose, the eldest. He is in Argentina now, breeding horses. The other two were just as bad. Horse mad."

Javier's uncle sought for words and failed.

"Give them my regards. Tell them from me that Argentina is far more healthy for them than France."

"Yes . . . no . . . I. . . ."

The door slammed and the officer and the men with him left. Minutes later the engine revved as the car backed over the rough ground and out between the farmyard gates.

The tension and fear and then the unspeakable relief had been to much. I leant my head back against the wall and began to laugh helplessly.

Chapter Fifteen

Minutes later Javier's uncle was grinning up at us wiping the beads of perspiration from his forehead.

"Mon Dieu, I wouldn't want to go through all that again."

"You were magnificent," Javier said generously. "I couldn't have done better myself."

His uncle cuffed him. "You couldn't have done it at *all*."

My legs, weak as a new-born kitten's, I climbed down the ladder, Romero and Jose behind me.

Javier's uncle stood, legs apart, hands on his hips, aglow with satisfaction.

"There is some good stew warming . . . and some beer. A bit early in the day perhaps, but we need it. I need it. All you had to do was keep quiet . . . if it wasn't for my presence of mind and courage. . . ."

"You mean if it wasn't for the French officer," Javier said cheekily.

His uncle slammed the soup ladle in his hand down onto the table, and with a roar of anger chased him round the room, the dog barking and joining in, knocking chairs over. Javier's yells of protest increasing the pandemonium. At last, after giving his nephew a vigorous box around the ears, his uncle returned to the stew.

"The Frenchman helped a little," he said condescendingly. "But only out of respect for me. . . ."

Javier laughed derisively again, to be quelled by a brandished spoon and indignant glare.

"Who was he?" I asked Jose.

"Felix Sastre. His father and my father were business

acquaintances. Felix is younger than me, he was just entering school as I left, so we never knew each other very well."

"Then why. . . ."

"His mother lost her reason shortly after the birth of her last child. She was put in a mental hospital at Pau. Her husband could not afford a private nursing home. My father visited her there and what he saw upset him terribly. He insisted that she was taken away and cared for in better surroundings. He knew that pride would forbid the Sastre's accepting money, and so he offered Felix's father a job at a ridiculously high salary on the mutual but unspoken understanding that it would pay the fees for a private nursing home. And," he said, his arm around me. "I'm very glad he did so. Otherwise you may have had to shoot your friend in the other foot as well!"

"Don't remind me," I said feelingly. "My only consolation is that at least I know he's had medical attention and isn't still tied to a chair in the cottage."

"You worry too much," said Javier, who blatantly never worried about anything. "I wish he *was* still tied and in the cottage. Not searching the countryside for us. How are we to reach Beyonne with that buffoon and his men lying in wait for us?"

"With great difficulty," Romero said, ladling the steaming hot stew onto his plate.

"But we *are* in France now." I said.

"Not far enough, Alison. The Spanish police have operated this side of the border before now." Romero looked glum. "And besides, as far as the officer is concerned, it's now a personal thing. Twice he has been made to look a fool in front of his men. . . ."

"That wasn't hard to do, was it?" Javier said gustily, ladling a second helping onto his plate. "The man is an idiot."

"Idiot or not he could still have us behind bars before the day is out," Romero said, determined to look on the black side.

"What do we do?" I asked Jose.

"I'm not sure. Leo. . . ." Javier's uncle turned. "Who lives in the adjoining cottages?"

The big man shrugged. "An elderly couple, and Ricardo and his wife and daughters."

"How old are the daughters?"

"Nineteen or twenty. They work in Bayonne and only come home in the holidays. I saw them yesterday, so I know they are here at the moment."

"Anybody else?"

"A young couple moved into the old Anavaros property. They have three children, but very young. Not yet at school."

"Good," Jose said thoughtfully. "And how far is it before the road reaches other houses?"

"Not till the village, two miles further down. Then a further mile out of the village it connects with the main coast road."

"I'm quite sure Felix will see to it that our friends don't hang around the farm, waiting for us to leave. But it will be out of his hands if they try to apprehend us on the road, out of the village. And they will. They know the horses are too tired to ride again, and the only other way out of here is by road."

"There is my car," Leo said, "A little old but still she goes."

"Thanks, Leo. But with only one road to worry about they will be able to watch the cars very carefully."

"And they will," Romero said with finality. "We won't be the first people the Spanish police have taken unwillingly back into Spain."

"They are not going to take us," Jose said confidently. "Come with me, Leo. The rest of you finish off the stew and have a rest." The amber-gold eyes were alight with amusement. "And don't worry Romero. When we leave, we will leave in style."

The door slammed behind him and Javier, Romero and myself stared at each other.

"It's been too much for him," Javier said at last. "He's mad."

"I hate to say it about a blood relation," Romero said. "But I think you're right. You heard the way the officer spoke to Sastre. He has sworn to see Jose dead and he means it."

"He said he'd see Villada dead. Perhaps one brother is as good as another." Javier said teasingly.

Romero threw a piece of bread at him. "He would like to see us all dead. You included."

The dog thumped its tail on the floor and then leapt up for the flying bread.

"You weren't much help," Javier said to it as he fended it off. "You never even snapped at them." The dog sniffed at the bread disdainfully and then eyed Javier's plate. Javier set it down on the floor and the dog finished the stew off, wagging his tail appreciatively.

"What sort of guard dog is that?" Javier asked in despair. "His master leaves him alone with three strangers in the house and all he does is eat."

"He did growl." I said.

"Nonsense. He's too lazy to even growl. He's like uncle Leo, all bluff and bluster."

"All bluff and what!" his uncle roared from the doorway.

"I said he was as fierce as you, uncle." Javier said, leaving the table hurriedly and standing behind Romero's chair.

"You ignorant cub!" his uncle bellowed. "What did my sister do to deserve a son like you. Bluff and bluster indeed. At least I don't have to travel France like a woman."

Javier stared at him. "A what?" he asked, as if he hadn't heard right.

Leo laughed, straddling a chair. "A woman! Mon Dieu, I'm glad I've lived long enough to see this day."

"They are both mad," Javier said to Romero, staring from his uncle to Jose and back again.

Jose threw some clothes onto the table. "Not mad. The neighbours have lent us these. Climb your way into them."

With growing horror Javier lifted up petticoats and skirts. "You don't mean it . . . it's a joke. . . ."

"And the joke is on you," his uncle crowed gleefully. "Come on Javier, see what a pretty woman you make."

"Never," Javier said, his cheeks flushing. "Romero, put that thing down."

Romero struggled ungainly into a blouse. "If this is the only way to leave then I'm taking it."

With a groan of pain Javier held up a skirt. "I can't. I'll never live it down. . . ."

"Get into it and stop complaining," Jose said. "You can't possibly look as bad as me."

He was right. He couldn't. Leo wiped a tear away from his eye as he rocked with laughter.

"Saints preserve us," he said. "If you could see your-selves. . . ."

Jose was barefoot with sandals on, an ankle length blue needlecord skirt and white blouse, his hair brushed into a fringe, with a polka dot scarf tied over his head, tying at the nape of his neck. Blue eyeshadow and mascara completed the picture and he was struggling to make Romero look less like a concert hall turn and more like a creditable woman. Javier was superb. A floral dress and strappy sandals were done justice to by a wig. He had been braver than Jose and his lips gleamed prettily beneath pink lipstick.

"You as well," Jose said, turning to me. There is a headsquare and sunglasses. You and Romero go in Ricardo's car. Javier and myself will go in Leo's."

"Dear heaven, will it work?"

"The car? Yes."

"The *clothes!*"

"They had better," Jose said, smoothing his skirt. "They will only see us from a distance, and they will be looking for three men and a girl. They shouldn't give us a second glance."

"A pity," Leo said. "Because you are worth it." He collapsed in laughter again, while Javier prinked in the front of a mirror.

"If your mother could see you now. . . ."

"Never mind my mother," Javier said, patting at his wig. "Who else is going to see me? If you think I'm driving all the way to Bayonne like this, you're wrong."

"Your clothes are in the boot," Jose said reassuringly. "Just be careful you don't get picked up by any strange men. . . ."

Javier glared at him murderously. "Any more wisecracks like that. . . ."

Jose and Javier got into Leo's car, Javier at the wheel. He really did look very feminine, the wig softening and changing his fine-boned face, the delicate mouth gleaming provocatively.

The same could not be said of Jose. My lover fluttered blue coated lashes at me, and said, "See you in Bayonne."

"Bayonne," I said like a prayer. "Bayonne."

Chapter Sixteen

We waited ten minutes and then followed after them. Romero at the wheel. Out through the gates, onto the unmade road, past the cottages, and down towards the village.

It was a lovely morning. As we neared the village we passed pleasant farmhouses with low red roofs and white plastered walls, cascades of honeysuckle and clematis clinging around the doors. The surrounding fields and meadows rolled undulating away to merge into forested slopes of pines and here and there turbulent streams swept down, rushing beneath stone bridges only just wide enough for our car to go over. The cornfields reached right up to the edge of the village houses, shifting like a golden sea in the light breeze. The road curled down, exchanging beaten earth for bumpy cobbles as it wound through the centre of the village. Here, the road ran straighter, between bakers and butchers, wine bars and tanneries. A tiny church, the plaster saint outside it garlanded by flowers, had a slender golden spire soaring up against the sun-filled sky.

The street was filled with shopping women, wicker baskets over their arms as they queued for fresh vegetables or stood in groups laughing and talking, stepping out of our way as we crawled along the crowded street at a snail's pace. There was no sign of the Spanish police, but then Jose had said that if they were waiting for us, it wouldn't be in full view of the villagers, but further along on the country road, away from curious eyes. We had to pause again as a crowd of children thronged the street, their school books in their hands. The morning sun was growing hotter and I wound my window down, my eyes searching, yet dreading to see, Martinez and Amiano and their vengeful officer. The cluster of houses and shops thinned, we passed the school with its shingled roof, its large bell ringing as the children trouped towards it, and then the village was behind us, and in front was the mile of deserted road before it joined the main road leading to the coast.

If the Spanish police were still intending taking us forcibly back to Spain, it would be on this next mile that they would do it. The verges of the road were thick with marguerites and every now and then an oak tree cast waving shadows and my tension increased. Behind each tree I imagined the Spanish officer, seething with rage, foaming for revenge. Faintly, the school bell still rang, and the road ahead remained deserted. There was no sign of Jose and Javier.

"I think," Romero said quietly. "I can see them."

My stomach muscles tightened painfully. Ahead of us on the left hand side, oak and beech grew closely together, and emerging from the density of the tree trunks, was the black bullet nose of a car. I took a deep breath and turned to Romero chattily, averting my head. The shadow of the tree darkened our car momentarily and then we had passed them and there was no sign of them following, only the sweet smell of grass and wild flowers and a wasp zooming uncomfortably near.

Romero glanced into his driving mirror. "It's them all right," he said, "And they're not moving."

Slowly my breathing returned to normal. I sank back against the leather of the car seat.

"Thank God," I said, and meant it.

The rough road joined the smooth surface of the main one and Romero picked up speed. The sun glittered down on the fields that edged the road, and sleek brown cattle grazed peacefully, swinging their tails to disturb the flies that settled on their backs. A mile went by and then another. Slowly my eyes closed, and weary beyond belief I sank into sleep.

When I woke it was to find that we were on the outskirts of Bayonne. The streets were lined with tamarisk trees, formal gardens stretching out on either side, children were playing pelota and black bereted men sipped drinks around white and red chequered tables.

We motored leisurely over a wide river, the grey water swirling forcefully seawards.

Sleep fled and I was filled with a glorious surge of elation. Within minutes I would be reunited with Jose, and at last we would have some precious time to ourselves. Time to talk. To brush away the dark shadow of fear I felt whenever I thought of Carmen.

We turned off the road lined with pavement cafes, twisting and turning into a maze of side streets, growing gradually poorer and meaner. We began to slow down and I could hardly suppress the joy I was feeling. Besides my reunion with Jose, there would be Miss Daventry and I would know once and for all, that she was safe.

The houses were crammed together, tall and thin, with no flowers or trailing vines to soften their harsh, poverty stricken appearance. There were a few shops selling fruit and vegetables, and the litter of discarded cabbage leaves and thrown out over-ripe fruit smelt sourly in the mid-day heat. The house outside which we had stopped looked as mean and even more uncared for, than the others in the street.

With Romero in front of me, I mounted the flight of dirty steps that led to a peeling, sun-blistered door. As we waited for admittance I noticed for the first time that there was no sign of Miss Daventry's little car parked anywhere in the street. I felt a twinge of apprehension, but before I could bring it to Romero's attention, the door was opened and I stepped into a darkened corridor. Immediately there were shouts of greeting and vigorous handclasps and arms flung around Romero's shoulders, and I stood watching, unable to see Jose, feeling suddenly lonely. Enthusiastically the men appraised Romero in his skirt and blouse, protesting when he demanded his clothes and chance to change. Then Javier was pushing his way through the throng of men, still in his dress and make-up, but grotesque without his wig.

"Alison, Alison," he shouted, pulling me towards him, kissing me gustily on both cheeks. His hand firmly holding mine he dragged me forwards.

"Alison," he said, his arm warmly round my shoulders. "Here are our good friends, Antonio, Manuel and Eugenio."

I was seized bodily, kissed with even greater enthusiasm and then enmeshed between them all, half carried up the steep flight of stairs and into a sparsely furnished room. There was a large table and several uncomfortable looking wood chairs and a grey metal filing cabinet and stack upon stack of pamphlets. There was no Jose.

"Let go of her," Javier was saying to a large boned young man who had practically lifted me off my feet. "Alison has promised that I shall take her out tonight." He raised his arms, stretching high above his head. "A bath, a sleep, and then. . . ." He whirled me round by the waist. "And then, whoopee!"

I said. "Where is Jose?"

"He has gone for some food. He will be back shortly."

I fought my disappointment. "And Miss Daventry?" I asked, my first flickerings of doubt growing as I disentangled myself from Javier's all too firm embrace. But I couldn't be heard over the exclamations of admiration for the way we had defeated the police. Javier embellishing the story so that it sounded as if we had taken on the whole might of Spain single-handed.

Romero said. "Where is Luis?"

Manuel, the six footer, said. "He is next door, asleep.'

Romero's face paled. "You mean he is worse? What happened?"

"I mean he is next door asleep," Manuel repeated. "See for yourself."

Romero was already striding across the room, whilst Javier pulled up a chair, straddled it, arms leaning on the back, face suddenly tense. Romero flung the door open and from where I sat I could see a truckle bed and Luis's head on a surprisingly clean pillow. Romero crossed the room to him, obliterating my view. He bent his head low to that of his brother, and then stood, gazing down at him, whilst Luis still slept, his cheeks flushed like those of a child. Gently Romero backed away, closing the door softly behind him.

"Satisfied?" Manuel asked.

Romero nodded. "What sort of shape was he in when he arrived, and how did he arrive?"

"How did *they* arrive?" I cried out, unable to contain myself any longer. "Where is Miss Daventry?"

The three men looked at each other and then Manuel said soothingly. "When Jose comes back we will explain things to you."

Javier pushed a rickety chair in front of me and I sat down. Intuition told me I was going to need it.

"Alison," Javier began, his eyes troubled, and then Antonio interrupted him, lifting a bottle of wine from the bottom drawer of the filing cabinet.

"This calls for a celebration," he said. "Javier, find some glasses."

Wine was poured liberally, Javier washed his face free from make-up, and I still sat in my chair, wondering what it was that Javier had been about to tell me, my elation turning to anxiety.

"Will Jose be long?" I asked at last. Antonio beamed at me. "Drink up. You haven't touched your wine yet."

"Jose," I said again, sipping at the wine. "Will he be long?"

Romero stood at the window gazing down into the street. Javier had disappeared into Luis's room to change out of his dress.

"No," Antonio said, beaming down at me. "He has gone to meet Pedro and Carmen."

"Oh," I said, the wine turning rancid in my mouth. "I see."

Chapter Seventeen

Sitting in the bare room, surrounded by three men I barely knew, Romero still with his back to me gazing down into the street, and Javier getting changed, it seemed as if the brief sun-lit hours at Lindaraja had been nothing but a dream. Lindaraja was in ashes, and so it seemed was Jose's desire. Whilst I had rushed here, overjoyed at the thought of our reunion, he hadn't even waited for me. He had gone, his only thoughts being for Carmen. No wonder Javier had looked so troubled when I had asked for Jose. Poor Javier. If he could have softened the blow for me, I know he would have.

I drank my wine determined not to let my anguish show.

If I had believed love to be where none existed, no-one else should know of it but myself. I had, after all, still some pride left.

There was a sharp knock on the door and in my nervousness I spilt my wine, Manuel hastily wiping the chair and my dress, despite my protestations. Javier came back into the room, slim-hipped in a pair of jeans and yellow tee-shirt. I avoided his eyes. Javier knew me too well for me to disguise my feelings from him.

Running footsteps raced up the stairs and Jose burst into the room.

"Are they here yet?" he asked anxiously. "There is no sign of them over the bridge." He slammed the bread and rolls down onto the table, then, seeing me for the first time his lustrous eyes rested on mine and his tone changed. He said gently: "You must be tired."

I nodded, my smile answering his, my anxiety subsiding.

"No," Manuel said. "They are not here, but don't worry, there is still plenty of time." He took a roll, splitting it open, buttering it liberally.

"You must be hungry as well," Jose said, not looking at Manuel, but passing a still warm roll across the table to me, his hand holding mine for a brief, precious second. Then he turned to Manuel, the gentleness gone. "Well, what happened?"

Manuel coughed and said slowly. "I'm still not sure how they crossed the border. Luis directed the Englishwoman here, he was utterly exhausted by the time they reached here. He had lost a lot of blood. The Englishwoman was no security risk, that much Luis could tell us. She cleaned his leg and re-bandaged it and told us that as far as she knew, both you and the English girl had drowned. After settling Luis down and giving him some sleeping tablets, she insisted that she find out what had happened to you on the beach. She had, she said, to know for definite whether her friend was dead or alive. And if alive, how she could best help her. Antonio was all for keeping her here against her will, but you had trusted her with your brother, it seemed we could do no less than trust her ourselves."

"And?" Jose demanded as Manuel paused awkwardly. Manuel lowered his eyes to the table. Eugenio, lank black hair hanging low over his forehead, stared studiously out of the only window the room possessed and Antonio was looking anywhere but at Jose.

"Well?" Jose demanded again, thumping the table with his fist. "Where is she now?"

Their discomfort was only too apparent. Eugenio's cheeks looked suspiciously flushed and my heart hammered painfully as the silent seconds lengthened into moments.

Manuel cleared his throat and Javier's hand rested reassuringly on my shoulder.

"You know about the split with Garmendia?" Manuel ventured at last.

"To hell with Garmendia," Jose shouted, leaning menacingly over the table, grasping Manuel by the collar of his shirt. "*Where is the Englishwoman?*"

Javier's hand slipped over mine, tightening, as Manuel said half defiantly, half apologetically. "Garmendia has her."

"The hell he has!" Jose shouted, half lifting Manuel off his feet in his fury.

Romero pitched forwards, hauling Jose back, away from the half-choked Manuel.

"There was nothing we could do," Eugenio said, desperate eyes seeking Romero's. "We couldn't keep her here by force. Not after what she had done for Luis ... she had been gone for only an hour, if that, when we got a telephone call. The man on the phone didn't identify himself, but it sounded like Alphonso Cia. He said Garmendia had kidnapped her and that her car was parked in the Rue Theire a note left in her own handwriting as proof that their claim was genuine."

"But why?" I cried out, totally uncomprehending.

"For me," Jose said tightly. "That's right, isn't it, Eugenio. For me."

"I don't understand," I said, pressing my hands against my throbbing temples. "Why should Garmendia kidnap her?"

Jose said quietly. "This whole disaster, right from the beginning has been because Garmendia wanted rid of me. It was Garmendia who ruined the expedition from Bayonne to Miguelou. It was Garmendia who told the police Alison's name, and it was Garmendia who shot one of the police and let us be incriminated for it. And now he wants me to meet him, and if I don't he shoots the Englishwoman, right?"

Manuel nodded, his eyes shadowed. "He says he wants to talk to you. He wants you to hand over all ETA units in your control. He wants you out of the country and unless you acquiesce. ..."

"He executes Miss Daventry."

Manuel nodded, looking nervously in my direction. "He believes you have a passion for the English girl and that the old woman is her aunt, and that for her sake you will agree to meet him."

"*Fool!*" Jose said forcefully, running his fingers through his hair. "Of all the stupid, idiotic, crazy. ..."

Romero turned from the window and said with a shrug. "Jose is leaving the country anyway. The expedition from Bayonne was to be the last thing he would do."

"Is that true?" Antonio asked, watching Jose closely.

Jose nodded. "My home is in Argentina, not Spain. I came here because I was asked, and I stayed to help because everything was deteriorating so rapidly. But I never meant it to be permanent. Once I had reorganised things to my satisfaction I intended going home. Back to my ranch and my horses. Lindaraja is burned to the ground now, there is nothing left to hold me in Spain any longer."

"But Miss Daventry?" I asked. "What about Miss Daventry?"

His eyes held mine and the expression in them made my body ache. "Don't worry, little one," he said tenderly. "We will free her." He turned to Manuel. "Where does Garmendia want me to meet him?"

Manuel passed him a letter. "This was the note we found in the car."

"Cotanes? I've never heard of it. What is it, a village?"

"It's a hamlet on the French side of the mountains. By car about two hours away."

"Make me some coffee," he said curtly to Eugenio. "Then I'm going."

"But you can't!" Manuel managed at last. "From Cotanes they can see you coming from miles away. They will easily know if you are alone or not. And Garmendia will not be alone. For heaven's sake man, to go there is to commit suicide."

"I'm no fool," Jose said wearily. "But I'm not going to let the Englishwoman die at the hands of two depraved psycopaths. Not after what she did for Luis."

Antonio opened his mouth to speak, looked at me and thought better of it. I could see the dawning expression in his eyes. He was beginning to think there was truth in what Angel had said. That Jose *did* love me. The reassurance warmed and sustained me.

"You need sleep," Romero said to his brother, but Jose said simply. "I will sleep in the car on the way there."

I looked at his face, deep lines etched in by pain and weariness and said desperately. "Must you go? Is there no other way?"

We looked at each other, oblivious of the others in the room. "Yes," he said. "I must. But it will not take long."

Romero drank his coffee putting the cup back on the table, saying in a firm voice. "I will drive Jose to Cotanes."

"Fool!" Manuel said without contempt. "You have not slept either. I will drive."

"He is my brother," Romero said, and Manuel's eyes slid defeatedly away from him down onto the floor.

"Garmendia insists you go alone," Antonio reminded him, leaning back in his chair, crossing his legs and propping them on the corner of the table.

"So I shall," Jose said, filling his gun with a fresh magazine of bullets. "Romero will drop me off a half mile away and I will walk the rest."

Eugenio shook his head. "You're mad. You're walking into a trap a child of three would avoid. Cotanes is set on a hill," he steepled his fingers descriptively. "There is nothing around it but fields and meadows. Not even woods. Nothing to afford shelter of any kind. Garmendia and Cia will be able to see you coming from miles away and as soon as they see you leave the car, they will shoot you down. And for what?" he spread his palms uppermost. "The Englishwoman will be dead by now. . . ."

Jose was hardly listening to him, from outside there came the faint sound of a car approaching, and then a slight jarring noise as it halted beneath the window. Eugenio and Manuel moved fast, at the window before I had even registered the car's approach. Their tenseness relaxed as they turned away, heading for the door and stairs.

"More visitors?" Antonio asked, his feet still lazily crossed and resting on the edge of the table.

"Pedro and Carmen," Manuel replied.

Javier grabbed my wrist as I let out a small cry and Jose, eyes brilliant, dashed from the room, hurtling down the wooden stairs.

Chapter Eighteen

"Take it easy, take it easy," Javier said, trying to restrain me as I ran across to the window. A weak sun struggled through banks of cloud to warm the street and shine on the stationary, shabby car at the kerbside below. Pedro's bulky figure was clearly visible at the wheel, but it was not Pedro I was interested in.

Agitatedly I leaned against the glass, straining to see Jose emerge from the doorway of the house. Simultaneously the car door opened and Carmen stepped out, shaking her long hair away from her face, straightening up as Jose raced across the pavement and swept her up in his arms.

Javier's hand gripped my shoulder tightly as the strength left my body and I almost fell against him. I had forgotten how beautiful she was. How dark and vibrant. Jose pushed her away from him, holding her at arms length, his eyes travelling her body from head to foot as if he could never get enough of the sight of her. Her dress was of scarlet cotton, clinging closely over the high, firm breasts, the narrow waist. Her hair hung, gleaming and glossy black, swinging as Jose hugged her closely to him again. I turned away, Javier's arm still holding me, and leant back against the wall for support.

Somehow I had to live through the next few minutes, their feet were on the steps now, hurrying upwards. I took a deep breath and with legs that felt as if they belonged to someone else. I walked back towards the table and sat down. I had not been an actress, however poor, for nothing. As they burst into the room, arms around each other, faces alight, Pedro immediately behind them, I smiled. Coolly and collectedly. Somehow I returned Carmen's embrace, saw her return to Jose, clasp his hand and then make her way over to the room where Luis lay sleeping. Jose was only feet away from me, I closed my eyes. This hell would not endure forever. Soon they would be gone and I would be able to weep and suffer in privacy, till then I had my pride. . . .

Pedro's ruddy face was wreathed in smiles, his black beret at a jaunty angle, his paunch straining beneath a too tight belt.

Arms outspread he swept me from my chair, whirling me round and round the room, singing; "We made it! We made it! Didn't I tell you it would be easy? Ah, your courage matches your beauty . . . and your brains. . . ." he released me suddenly, flinging his beret in the air, slamming his fist on the table.

"Where are the drinks then? At least some wine Eugenio, you peasant you. . . ."

"Roque is dead," I heard Eugenio say quietly as I struggled to keep my eyes from Jose's. "And Garmendia is holding the other Englishwoman hostage at Cotanes. Romero and Jose are going to free her."

I was aware of Pedro's immediate deflation, of him sitting heavily on one of the chairs, his head in his hands, calling on the saints for help, chastising them for their injustice, but I was more aware of the swirl of Carmen's skirts returning into the room, brushing against the black leather of Jose's boots.

"You must allow me to come with you," Javier was saying to Jose. "You owe it to me."

"I owe you nothing," I heard Jose say briskly, my eyes determindly downcast. "Certainly not your death."

And then he was walking out of the room and agonised I raised my eyes. Romero was in front of him, Javier was still protesting, and Carmen, as if he were going on an errand no more dangerous than to the shops, was walking towards Luis's room, Eugenio and Manuel watching her swaying hips in silent approval. I jumped to my feet, forgetting all my intentions of salvaging my pride, running down the steep flight of stairs after them.

"Jose!" I called breathlessly. "Jose!"

It was too late. The car was already speeding away, leaving me in a cloud of dust and dirt and exhaust fumes. I stood, hands hanging limply by my side, knowing that it was over and that somehow I had to accept it. But as I turned to Javier, my face wet with tears, I knew that as long as I lived I would never forget amber-gold eyes gazing deep into mine, and seeing in those gold-flecked depths only joy and pleasure in the holding of me, and for however brief a period of time, love.

The street was empty now and silent. Javier touched my arm gently and led me unseeingly back up the flight of steps. I was unable to think of anything beyond the fact that Jose had gone and that he was going to be killed.

Eugenio poured fresh coffee into my cup and I sat down, hands wrapped around it, trying to think clearly, to understand. The coffee was good, hot and strong and reviving. But I could think of nothing, only that Jose had gone and that there was no means for me to follow him, and that he no longer wanted me anyhow. Carmen was still with Luis and I kept my eyes averted from the door, dreading the moment that she would come out and join us.

"Don't worry," Javier said, sitting on the edge of the table, his face, for once, unsmiling. "Jose is no fool. He will have a plan all ready in his head. He will walk into no trap set by Garmendia."

I remained silent, unconvinced. The inner door opened and Luis, tousel-haired and still half asleep, limped into the room. On seeing me, his dark eyes widened and then his face creased in a sudden, joyous smile.

"Alison! Alison! You're here. How the devil did you manage it, and where is Jose?"

For the first time my eyes met Carmen's. She stood behind him, shrugging her shoulders helplessly as if the pain of telling him had been too much for her. Luis gazed dazedly round the room.

"We arrived about half an hour ago," Javier said. "Over the mountains, via my own private route, though I doubt if I will ever be able to use it again!"

"And Jose?" Luis repeated. "Where is Jose?"

I took a deep breath. "He's gone to meet Angel Garmendia," I said, my heart lurching as I saw joy in his eyes, so like Jose's, fade and die.

"*Garmendia?*" Luis asked, sitting down abruptly. "But Garmendia wants to kill him."

"Garmendia is holding Miss Daventry hostage."

"I see," he said, his face paling. "And Romero?"

"Romero has gone with him."

"And they let me sleep on, without even saying goodbye!" his voice was incredulous.

"There was no point," I said gently. "You would only have wanted to go with them, and if you had you would have been a hindrance to Jose in your condition."

"And is his condition so much better?" Luis asked stonily.

I swallowed, trying to keep my voice steady, all too aware of Carmen listening and watching. "His wound was not as severe as yours, Luis. And Javier is confident that Jose will take no risks and that he knows what he is doing."

"But to risk his life for an elderly foreigner he has only known three days ... it doesn't make sense."

"She risked an awful lot to help you," I said gently. Luis looked abashed.

"Nothing makes sense anymore," he said again.

Silently I agreed with him. Three short days ago I had never even met Jose Villada. Now he filled all my thoughts waking and sleeping. He had entered my life like a flaming comet, burning me with love, and he had gone from my life as dramatically as he had arrived. And even while the girl he was going to marry stood only feet away from me, I knew I loved him still. That I always would.

I said quietly. "No, nothing makes sense anymore."

Pedro had joined Manuel, Antonio and Eugenio at the far end of the table. They were bent over it, studying a large, fraying map. Javier stood apart, his face thoughtful, his brow furrowed. He put one foot on a chair, resting his hand on one knee, cupping his chin. "Well?"

The men at the table straightened their backs and faced him.

"It's entirely up to you and Pedro ... if you want to risk it."

"Risk what?" I cried, standing up hastily, the chair clattering as it fell backwards.

"We're going to Cotanes," Javier said. "I don't believe for one minute that Angel is waiting there with only Alphonso Cia and the Englishwoman for company. Nor that he only wants to persuade Jose to relinquish leadership of the Spanish side of ETA. He wants him dead. And," he said, picking up his jacket and swinging it over one shoulder. "He isn't going to succeed, not if we can help it."

Manuel sent a bunch of car keys skittering across the table and Javier pocketed them, Pedro moving across the room, joining him.

My mouth was dry. I waited for Carmen to speak but she remained silent, composed. Suddenly I didn't care anymore. I had no room for anything but concern for Jose. Not even jealousy. That those dancing, laughing, desiring eyes of amber-gold should gaze down at Carmen. That he was hers by right as the diamond on her finger openly testified, seemed hardly to matter. All that mattered was that Jose should live. Please God, let him live, let him live, was the prayer that circled my brain, beating against the back of my eyes. I said: "I'm coming too."

Carmen made a noise of protest, moving up behind me. "There is no *point* in your going," she said.

I said again quietly: "I'm going."

I walked over to the head of the stairs. "Are you ready, Javier?" He looked across at Pedro. The big Spaniard shrugged his shoulders. "Miss Daventry is her friend and countrywoman. She knows the dangers. If she wishes to come, let her come."

The swirl of scarlet moved up beside me. "Why?" she asked innocently. I think, if I had turned to face her, that I would have told her the truth, that I loved Jose, that nothing in my life mattered but his safety. Pedro saved me from the scene that would have followed.

"Because of the old one," he said, patting Carmen on the head. "It is natural."

She grasped my hand. "She will be safe, Alison. Jose will save her." I knew by the tone of her voice that it had not been heartlessness that had prevented her from going with him, from behaving as I was now doing, only an implicit faith in her lover. In the sure knowledge that he would return to her. He would not be returning to me, and I knew with even more certainty that I had to go to Cotanes with Pedro and Javier, for it would be the last time I would have the chance to play any part in Jose's life.

I said: "I will feel better if I go, Carmen. Miss Daventry is old, and . . ." my voice faltered, unable to continue. She released my hand and blindly I followed Javier down the stairs, stumbling in my haste. Pedro's large hand checked my fall and guided me out into the street.

"Will we be able to make it in time?" Javier asked Pedro anxiously. Pedro shrugged. "This is an old car, she won't travel as fast as the one Jose and Romero took."

"How fast?" Javier asked, opening the car door.

"Thirty . . . thirty-five if the roads are good."

"The roads to Cotanes are like mud tracks," Javier said bluntly. "How long do you think it is since they left?" he turned to look at me as I slid along the back seat.

"About twenty minutes . . . not much longer." I had no real idea. The time spent in the claustrophobic little room, Jose totally lost to me, reunited with Carmen, had seemed endless.

Javier fitted the key into the ignition. "Then we had better hope this car improves its speed. Or we will be too late."

"No," I protested, my voice hoarse. "Don't say that! Please God, don't say that!"

Chapter Nineteen

We approached the village slowly, the rain leaving the steeply winding road that led to it, a quagmire. The village seemed empty. As we motored slowly down the main street a man stood in the doorway of an inn, glass in hand. He was fat and bull-necked and eyed us with hostile curiosity.

With mounting tension, we parked the car and approached the inn.

"Has Garmendia been here?" Javier asked.

"Garmendia?"

"Angel Garmendia. The Basque separatist. You know who I mean."

"Yes," the barman said from the depths behind. "Yes, I know who you mean and he has been here."

"Has?" I croaked. "Has? Where is he now? Who went with him. Who. . . ."

"What about the Villada's?" Javier asked. "Have they been here?"

The heavy jowled man at the door shook his head. "You can take your feuds elsewhere. Don't drag Cotanes into it. We want no part of it."

"But what's *happened?*" I cried, taut nerves snapping at last.

"Ask your friend," he nodded in the direction of the bead curtain.

Disregarding Javier's warning I ran to the curtain and dragged it back. Beneath a magnolia tree, straw hat rammed firmly on her head, binoculars and camera intact, a drink in her hand, sat Miss Daventry.

"My dear Alison. I'm so glad to see you. And Javier and Pedro. How nice. Do sit down and have a drink."

"What," I said weakly. "Has happened? And where is Jose?"

"It's a long story," she said, pleased at having such a captive audience. "Do sit down and have some refreshment."

She was as resilient, as irrepressible as ever. Even Javier and Pedro were unable to rise to the occasion. Dumbly they did as she asked and we sat in a circle on the wicker chairs while Miss Daventry poured out generous glasses of wine and handed them round.

"Please," I said, hanging on to the last shreds of patience and sanity. "Where is Jose? Is he all right?"

"He was the last time I saw him, which was," she looked at her watch. "About half an hour ago."

"For heaven's sake, what happened? *Did* Garmendia kidnap you?"

"Oh, most definitely," she said cheerfully. "But really, Alison. You must have some patience. If I'm to tell you what has happened I must start from the beginning . . . though I'm not sure where that was," she added thoughtfully.

"As far as I'm concerned the beginning was when Jose and myself were nearly drowned and you and Luis were being fired on by the police."

"Coastguards, actually."

I took a deep, shuddering breath. "All right. Coastguards. Now *what* happened after that?"

Miss Daventry adjusted her hat, jamming a hatpin even more firmly through the crown and said:

"We escaped of course. No sense in hanging around with all those bullets flying through the air. I had all my documents on me and I simply drove straight to the border and crossed into France. I knew you would make for Bayonne. . . ."

"Luis," I said faintly. "You had Luis with you."

"Well, I expect luck was on our side, it being night you know, I simply stuffed him in the boot five minutes before the checkpoint and let him out five minutes after. All you really need when dealing with the police is a lot of patience and the ability to lie with conviction . . . I can never really understand it. Other people seem to have such trouble at frontiers, searches and all that, and insufferable delays. But they never seem to be able to get me through fast enough. I can't imagine why."

I could, but I hadn't the heart to tell her.

"I must say it's all been very exciting, quite the most interesting holiday I've had for years." She beamed cheerfully at Pedro. "Those people in Bayonne. So nice and polite. Eugenio draws you know. Very talented. I told him he was wasting his time fighting governments. Much more sensible to accept things as they are and get on with enjoying life. . . ."

"And then you went for a walk?" I said, the words strangling in my throat.

"Ah yes. Now this is the interesting part. I was walking down the Rue d'Espagne . . . or was it the Rue Faures . . . I really can't remember. Anyway, I was making my way towards the cathedral when a car drew up beside me and someone called my name." She paused dramatically. "It was Garmendia. He said he had kidnapped both you and Jose and that if I didn't go with him he would shoot both of you. Of course I didn't believe a word of it. The man must have thought me a simpleton. But I *did* think it an offer I couldn't refuse. I do *so* like being the centre of things . . . to know what is going on . . . so I got into the car and away we went."

"You didn't fight . . . struggle . . . ?" Pedro asked with an air of one who has given up all hope.

"No, I didn't," Miss Daventry said crossly. "I told you, I wanted to know what was going *on*. Alphonso Cia was in the car. And what a nasty piece of work *he* is. We drove straight here and it wasn't till then that I knew what he was going to do. Of course *then* I wished I hadn't been so rash, but it was too late to alter things. He told me quite frankly what he was going to do. He said Jose Villada was in love with you and that as I was your aunt . . . really, I can't imagine *where* he gets his information from . . . that by holding me as hostage he could lure Jose to Cotanes. And," she said, pouring some more wine into her glass. "Kill him. I must admit I wasn't too worried. After all I knew you weren't in love with Jose, I told Garmendia so. I must admit he began to look worried. And I had every faith in Jose. I knew he would have more sense than to walk into such a childish trap. So here we all waited. And I made plans."

"Plans?" Pedro asked faintly.

"Plans," Miss Daventry said firmly. "As I said, I was sure Jose would have more sense than to come to Cotanes ... and when Garmendia and Cia finally realised this I thought they might be quite annoyed, so I made plans. But of course," she said brightly, beaming at us all. "Since he *did* come, and since you are all here, all my escape plans were totally unnecessary."

"Please go on," Javier said, with a glazed look about his eyes.

"It was Cia's job to watch the road so that Angel would have plenty of warning. Well, he got a warning all right. But it wasn't Jose who was approaching Cotanes, it was a police car. The car turned towards the square and by that time of course Cia was back in the inn like a crazed lunatic. Blaming everything on to Garmendia and saying they would be arrested or shot and Garmendia telling him not to be such a fool and neither of them noticing me very much at all. I could see the two policemen leave their car and begin to walk towards the inn ... and so could Garmendia and Cia. For a shocking moment I actually thought they were going to shoot it out, but of course Angel is not a complete fool. To shoot a policeman gets you only one sentence in Spain. Death by garotting. And though Garmendia is undoubtedly a murderer, as far as I know, there is no direct evidence against him. Not so far as shooting policemen are concerned. Anyway ..." she took a deep breath. "Garmendia and Cia decided to bluff it out. They stood at the bar casually, with drinks in their hands, trying to look innocent and failing lamentably ... so of course, *they* didn't see."

She clasped her hands in her lap, gazing round at us with sunny geniality.

"See what?" I asked, my voice little more than a croak.

"Why, that the policemen were Romero and Jose! Though I didn't know it was Romero at the time of course ... such a nice man ... Spanish aristocracy at its best ... not," she said hastily, patting Pedro's knee, "meaning any reflection on you, my dear Pedro. No-one could be more of a gentleman than you."

"And ..." we all asked together, leaning forward. "And then what?"

"Ah, now comes the action. And what action! Haven't seen anything like it since nineteen thirty-seven. If we had had the Villada's with us then, Pedro, the whole course of the war could have been altered!"

Terrified that she was about to digress once more, I said carefully. "What ... happened ... then?"

"Really, Alison. There is no need to talk like that. I'm not a child you know. Or deaf. What happened was this. The Villada's stepped into the inn, walking slowly and steadily towards the bar and the turned backs of Garmendia and Cia. Then, so quickly that I hardly saw, they had whipped the men round, slamming their fists into their jaws sending them sprawling and snatching their guns from them. I've never seen anything quite like it before. It was quite extraordinary. Perfect co-ordination. With the guns out of the way it simply developed into a fist fight. I did skirt round them, picking up the guns they had slung across the floor. If either Garmendia or Cia had reached them it would have been the end. Then I stood in the doorway," she nodded in the direction of the swinging beaded curtain that led back into the inn, "and watched."

"Please," I said. "Where is Jose now. And Garmendia?"

"There you go again, Alison. Rushing things. Of course it was difficult to watch both sets of men fighting at the same time, so I concentrated on Jose, I was worried about his shoulder and if things had got sticky I would have had no hesitation in making use of one of the guns. German Walthers P38's," she said to Pedro. "I haven't used one since the war, felt quite strange having one in my hand again. . . . Anyway, Jose seemed to be doing quite all right without my help. Garmendia broke away from Jose's grasp and was glancing wildly round for his gun ... then Jose rushed him, sending him flying once more, but Garmendia was quick. He was back on his feet in seconds and gave Jose a really solid punch to the jaw ... but Jose didn't break away. They stayed locked together and I could see blood but I didn't know if it was Angel's or Jose's, and then Garmendia split Jose's lip and Jose kneed him in the groin and then they were both on the floor, and it was very hard to tell who was winning and who was losing. Garmendia was trying to get a firm hold of Jose's throat and I really thought I would have to intervene, but he twisted away, out of Garmendia's grasp and staggered to his feet again and then Garmendia kicked out at him and Jose fell on him, pinning him to the floor and Romero and Cia were already rolling around in the dust, locked so close together that I couldn't tell what was happening . . . and all the time that incredible barman just kept on polishing his glasses. There was an awful lot of grunting and swearing and cries of pain and then it did seem that Garmendia had the upper hand and was going to throttle Jose. Quite understandable . . . Jose having been so recently wounded," she explained kindly, "I began to walk across to them trying to keep out of Romero and Cia's way, they were swaying and falling all over the place . . . and then Garmendia was on his knees and Jose had his arm round his neck and I really think he would have strangled him then and there, but Garmendia heaved himself forward throwing Jose off balance and then ran from the inn and out into the street with Jose panting and running after him. I didn't see what happened then, as I dare not leave Romero who finally seemed to be weakening, but I heard Garmendia's car roar into life and seconds later Jose's car scream out of the street and down the hill, so I presumed that it was Jose chasing Garmendia . . . but by this time Romero was definitely getting the worst of it and I thought enough was enough. I had to yell quite loud to be heard, in actual fact I had to fire the gun before anyone would take any notice of me. I kept it levelled at Cia who seemed quite surprised . . . and then Romero struggled to his feet, and his face was dreadfully marked, he'll have the bruises for weeks, and with me pointing the gun at Cia he managed to tie his hands behind his back and gag him. Not that he could have called for help anyway. It was patently obvious that no-one in Cotanes was going to intervene, but his language was quite offensive."

"And where," Pedro asked. "Is Cia now?"

"Why, in the inn's cellars. Didn't I tell you? Romero's down there with him now, trying to find out where Garmendia may be making for."

"Holy saints," Pedro breathed devoutly. "Take us to him now, this very minute."

"There's no hurry," Miss Daventry said, petulent at losing her audience. "There's nothing more we can do."

"There is," I said tightly. "There is still Jose."

"Oh, he'll come to no harm," Miss Daventry said airily. "If ever a man can look after himself, that one can."

"The cellars," Pedro repeated, struggling for calm.

Miss Daventry rose to her feet, smoothing out the creases in her dress. "If you insist. Though I'm sure Romero will be coming back at any moment."

"We insist," Javier said.

She shrugged. "Very well then. Follow me."

We followed her back into the inn, passing the whole length of the zinc topped bar, ignoring the barman as he ignored us, and then through a narrow doorway and down into the gloom of a large cellar stacked high with cobwebby casks.

"Romero," Miss Daventry called out breezily. "We have company. Alison is here. And Pedro. And Javier."

There was a half-choked sigh of relief and then Romero was at the bottom of the steps looking unbelievingly up at us. His handsome face was streaked with dirt and sweat, a swelling bruise distorting his left cheek, the blood running from a cut lip, smearing stickily down over his chin, staining his shirt a ghastly red.

We moved back, allowing him to climb the stairs. I gave him an inadequate handkerchief and he dabbed at the still flowing blood.

"I can't get any sense from him," he said to Javier. "God alone knows where they are."

"How did you do it?" Javier asked. "How in the name of all that is wonderful, did you do it?"

Romero managed a sheepish grin. "We took a police car at gunpoint. Took their clothes *and* their car, and left them in their underwear, tied and bound, and as far from a main road as it is possible to get!"

Pedro threw his head back and laughed, slapping his paunch.

"Superb, my friend. Superb. And now, for all of us. A drink."

"Jose," I said for the hundredth time. "There is still Jose," then I stiffened as the faint sound of a car engine throbbed in the distance. We looked at each other, frozen into immobility.

Was it the police? Or Garmendia coming back for Cia after killing Jose? Or was it, please God . . . Jose?

I wasn't the only one who seemed unable to react. In the end it was Miss Daventry who said briskly. "Leave me a gun, just in case. The rest of you go down into the cellar."

It seemed as sensible a suggestion as any. The barman's face didn't flicker. As far as he was concerned he was seeing nothing, hearing nothing, and telling nothing.

The cellar smelt stale and damp, and with the door shut the darkness was total. I wondered where Alphonso Cia was, if he should free himself . . . if he should pounce upon us unawares and defenceless.

Over the heavy drumming of my own heartbeat I strained to hear what was going on above, every nerve stretched, waiting for the vibration of other footsteps. . . .

Minutes passed and still nothing happened. We were crammed together and I could feel the damp perspiration that was soaking Javier's shirt and the faint smell of garlic on Pedro's breath.

I heard the faint click of footsteps upon stone, and then footsteps, but more than those of one person. It couldn't be Jose. It was the police . . . my whirling brain tried to think straight. We were in France now. Surely that meant we had nothing to fear? Surely the Spanish police couldn't operate so far beyond the frontier? Or was it the French police? Could we be extradited? I began to feel sick, longing for fresh air.

The door above us opened, and the next few seconds lasted an eternity. Then I was following Javier out into the stone floored room, gazing uncomprehendingly at Eugenio.

Chapter Twenty

"Thank goodness . . ." I began, and then my legs buckled under me, weak with relief. Javier caught hold of me, pressing me down onto a chair, saying: "Don't faint now. Not for Eugenio's sake!"

Briefly, far more briefly than Miss Daventry, Javier told him what had happened. Eugenio gazed open-eyed at the indomitable Miss Daventry.

"And we still have no idea where they have gone. . . ." Javier finished.

Eugenio still seemed lost for words. "Tut, tut," Miss Daventry said, giving his shoulder a shake. "Have you lost your ability to speak? What we need now is a bit of action!"

"Haven't you had enough of that already?" Javier asked dazedly.

She ruffled his hair as if he were a boy of ten. "You don't know the meaning of the word. One day, when we have time, I'll tell you what it was like in nineteen thirty-six and seven. And about Guernica too. Alison is quite right. What matters now is Jose."

"Tell me slowly, once again, what happened," Pedro said, his black eyebrows meeting together as his brow furrowed in thought.

"Garmendia ran. He reached his car and I heard it screech round the corner and then seconds later Jose took the police car they had so shrewdly obtained, and hared off after him."

"But where to?" I asked distractedly, staring round at the blank circle of faces, "In which direction would he have gone?"

Eugenio said quietly. "I passed no-one on the road leading to Cotanes, so that means they must have branched off onto the first main road. I could follow. I came here on Antonio's motor-bike and it's pretty fast, but I don't think there's much chance of catching them up. They could have turned right or left at the main road, who knows? And if Jose has already caught up with Garmendia, I'd be too late to be of help anyway."

Even Romero's shoulders sagged in agreement. With strained faces they sat down on the scattered bar stools, and the imperturbable barman poured ice-cold beer into glasses. I stared down into mine, feeling utterly helpless. To have come all this way, the tension within me mounting with every passing minute, and now, nothing. Nothing to do but wait. I stood up, the glass still held in my hands, striding the floor first one way and then another. There must be something we could do ... anything would be better than this nerve destroying inactivity.

Javier walked across to me. "I think perhaps we need to talk, Alison. A lot has happened and I think you need some things explaining to you. I wondered before, but back in Bayonne I became sure. Let's find some privacy."

I followed him across the room and out through the rustling curtain into the courtyard, dazzling white in the heat of the sun, all traces of mist and rain far away. I felt Miss Daventry's eyes following me, openly interested. It was obvious she now knew I was in love with Jose. But did she know how much? Could anyone ever know how much?

Please God, I prayed silently. Please let him be alive. Please let him come striding through the doorway big and strong, his hair in a knot of tangled curls, his eyes sparkling with laughter. . . .

Javier took my hand. "It's been a hell of a week for all of us," he said, and ridiculously I began to cry. "So much has happened that I think perhaps you and Jose have been taking things a little too much for granted."

I turned my head away staring resolutely at a peacock butterfly dancing amongst the wisteria blossoms as Javier led me to a seat beneath the heavy scent of a magnolia tree. Here it comes, I thought. Kind friend spelling things out clearly for me. Not wanting me to make a fool of myself any longer.

I said. "It's all right, Javier. I know. I knew in Bayonne. But I chose to come here for my own reasons. I knew my coming wouldn't make the situation any different. As soon as I know that Jose is safe I shall leave."

"There you are!" Javier said, one foot up on the wicker bench beside me, gazing down at me his dark eyes full of concern. "You're still not listening to me, are you? How do you think Jose would feel if, as soon as we knew he was still alive, you raced straight across France for home?"

"Relieved, I should think," I said with an effort at a laugh. "I'm sorry, Javier. I know he would want to see me, to thank me, to say goodbye properly, but I don't want it that way." I pushed a tracery of leaves away, plucking at a fallen magnolia blossom, my voice shaking a little, despite my desperate efforts at self control. "I couldn't bear it. I've seen him leave me once. To ask me to do it again is too much." I looked helplessly at him, willing him to understand. "I love him, Javier. I shall not have the strength to turn round and leave him, without betraying my feelings. And I've too much pride for that."

"Alison, Alison," Javier said gently, sitting down beside me, taking my hand once more. "Is it because of Carmen?"

I let the petals scatter to the ground, not trusting myself to speak, just nodding my head.

"Carmen," Javier said, speaking slowly and clearly, "is engaged to Luis."

The words seemed to hang forever in the sweet-ladened air.

"To Luis," I repeated faintly.

"To Luis," Javier said firmly. "They have been sweethearts since childhood."

The butterfly ventured nearer, flickering round the edge of the leaves.

"But I thought. . . ." The courtyard was spinning, whirling round me and Javier was steadying me, saying with a laugh.

"I know what you thought, idiot. But not till I saw your reaction when Carmen arrived in Bayonne and Jose went to meet her."

"You mean there is nothing between them . . .?" I could hardly breathe, my chest felt as if it were bursting.

"There's something between them all right," Javier said cheerfully.

"A bond that goes back to childhood, and the knowledge that very soon they will be brother and sister-in-law."

"Oh," I said inadequately, the strength flooding back into my body, my joy so great I could hardly contain it.

"And of course there is something else I thought I ought to mention to you whilst I have the chance."

"Yes," I said eagerly. "Yes?"

"That Jose loves you."

A glorious sweep of elation surged through me. Jose did love me, and nothing or anyone stood between us. I was overjoyed the whole world bright again. Rich and glittering and full of promise. Jose. *Jose.* . . .

Chapter Twenty-one

I ran into the inn, pushing the beaded curtain away hastily.

"Good gracious!" Miss Daventry said. "What on earth has Javier been saying to you?"

I grasped her hands, eyes shining. "You made a mistake. Back in Miguelou, you made the most awful, wonderful, mistake."

"Has she taken leave of her senses?" Miss Daventry asked Javier over the top of my head.

"No, I've regained them. Listen, do you remember, that first night in Miguelou, when the boat was fired on?"

"It's hardly a thing that would have slipped my memory considering the circumstances we all find ourselves in."

"I asked you if there were any local men on board and you said four. Among them Luis and Jose Villada. You said quite distinctly that Jose was Carmen's fiance."

"Did I dear?" Miss Daventry asked vaguely. "How foolish of me, but I'm sure I don't remember. Was it important?"

"*Yes*, because, don't you see? I fell in love with Jose and all the time I thought it was hopeless because he was going to marry Carmen!"

Miss Daventry sighed. "And you mean to tell me that in the past three days when you have spent so much time together, you never asked the man straight out?"

"It wasn't as easy as you think," I said spiritedly. "We were hardly ever alone together, and besides I was waiting for *him* to tell *me*. After the way he greeted her in Bayonne I didn't think there was any question of it. I thought I'd been mistaken about his feelings for me."

"You young people never cease to amaze me," Miss Daventry said, shaking her head. "All this liberation of the sexes and it seems to get you nowhere. If I had been in your position I would have known how the land lay straight away. I remember in nineteen thirty-six when I was in love with General Ria. . . ."

"Jose could still be dead." Romero interrupted her brutally.

I turned, the blood draining from my face. In the ecstasy of knowing he loved me, I had forgotten everything else.

"Oh God, what can we do?" I asked him. "We must do something. We can't just sit here, waiting."

Romero drummed his fingers on the bar. "They've been gone a long time now."

"Not if they were both in cars and Garmendia managed to stay ahead." Eugenio said, pushing his hair away from his eyes.

"Aren't you forgetting something?" Javier asked quietly. The men sat on their bar stools, watching him intently. "Garmendia is no fool. I'm not so sure he would run from Jose."

Silence hung, unbroken except for the drumming of Romero's knuckles.

"You mean you think Garmendia deliberately raced off in the car, leading Jose away from Cotanes?" Eugenio asked.

Javier nodded.

"Then if he did that," I said, my mouth dry. "It means Garmendia knew where he was going . . . and knew that when he had duped Jose into following him, that he would be able to kill him."

"Yes," Javier said miserably. "It does."

Romero shook his head, toying with his glass. "I don't think so, Javier. Remember, Garmendia and Cia thought they had it all tied up here. Jose and myself took them by complete surprise. I doubt if Garmendia would have had a reserve plan up his sleeve."

"I agree with Romero," Miss Daventry said. "As far as Angel and Alphonso knew, all that was needed was that Jose should arrive in Cotanes. Nothing else."

Javier sank back leaning against the wall, eyes closed.

"What made you come?" Pedro asked Eugenio suddenly. "You said we were fools to follow Jose here."

"You were," Eugenio said, holding his glass between his knees. "And so am I for changing my mind and coming as well. Just put it down to my better nature ... and the fact that another bomb went off in Bilbao an hour ago. I know it couldn't have been Garmendia himself, but he was behind it. The whole movement is breaking up and moving into chaos. Have Garmendia free another week and we will be back to the same position we were in two years ago. Plus the fact that the only separatists not rounded up and being held in jail are the maniacs that have gone over to Garmendia. I sometimes wonder if he has the police themselves in his pocket."

Romero said dryly. "Not even Garmendia could manage that. Not on a big enough scale anyway. He's had the luck of the devil this last week."

"You can say that again," Javier said bitterly. "All our men arrested within twenty-four hours, or as many as makes no difference, and Garmendia and his mob rampaging the countryside from Bilbao to Bayonne, and still free."

"I wonder," said Miss Daventry, her face grave. "I wonder. ..."

"Yes?" I prompted. "Go on."

"Jose was driving the police car wasn't he? I was just wondering how far he would be likely to get on main roads in a stolen police car."

Romero swore. "Not bloody far ... why the hell didn't I think of it. ..."

I let out my breath slowly. "You mean you think the police have picked him up and that Garmendia has got away?"

"It would account for neither of them returning," Javier said, opening his eyes, his face pale.

I swallowed hard. "And if they have ... what will happen to him?"

Eugenio said after a few seconds silence. "It depends on the amount of collaboration between the French and Spanish police forces."

"But the French policeman at the farm wouldn't let the Spaniards search for us!"

"He was also a friend," Eugenio said cynically. He stubbed his cigarette out and lit another. "A month ago a Spanish policeman, heavily armed, was shot twenty-five miles inside French territory by a separatist he was chasing. The policeman was called Azores and came from Madrid. He was taken to hospital for treatment and then escorted by the Spanish consul in Bayonne and the French security police back to the border. Later it was officially confirmed that Azores had had several companions. Two cars were also found deep within French territory. One containing a sub-machine gun and ammunition, the other car containing photographs of people alleged to be members of ETA and living in France. I mention this for two reasons. First, because it was important to us, as Basques, because though we have known about illegal Spanish police activity for years beyond the border, this was the first officially reported case. That is the reason the French are playing it cool at the moment. They don't want another public incident. Secondly, because it proves that the Spanish police are quite used to crossing the border after their quarry. If the Spanish officer and his men who chased you to the farm are still anywhere in the vicinity, then Jose will be forcibly taken back to Spain. . . ."

"And?"

"The sentence for killing a policeman is death by garotting." Romero said, eyes anguished.

"*But he hasn't killed one!*" I protested hysterically. "He hasn't killed anyone!"

"According to Spanish news sources he has," Javier said gently. "And so have you."

I grasped his hand, sick and shivering. Eugenio crushed his half smoked cigarette beneath his heel.

"I'm going to look for them. I'll take the left hand turn at the main road."

"And I'll take the right," Romero said. "Javier, stay here and wait. One of them will return. Garmendia to collect Cia . . . or Jose to collect Miss Daventry."

I watched them go and then returned bleakly to the bar. Even Miss Daventry's usual optimism seemed to have waned. Pedro sat at the top of the cellar steps, apparently keeping an eye on Alphonso Cia, and the barman stared listlessly at us with uncaring eyes.

I said. "I can't stand here doing nothing. I'm going for a walk."

For a moment I thought Miss Daventry was going to suggest accompanying me and then I saw understanding in her eyes, and she said only: "Don't go too far away, Alison."

"I won't. I just want to be able to see the road, that's all."

I walked over the cobbles that led from the square, back towards the bend where it curved out of sight, circling the steep hillside, till it levelled out amidst green fields. I would be able to see him coming, and long before the car climbed slowly into Cotanes I would know if it was Jose approaching . . . or Angel Garmendia.

I sat down on the cool of a crumbling stone wall and commenced my vigil, wrapping my arms around my knees, hugging them to me, trying to control my deepening anxiety as the snake-like road far below me remained stubbornly bare.

We had driven into Cotanes from the west, as had Eugenio, and Eugenio had said that the road had been deserted. Was it from the east then, he would come?

The road meandered into the far distance, a heat haze hanging over it so that my eyes ached as I looked down on it, wanting only to see the police car he had driven off in, dreading to see anything else, anything that could possibly be Garmendia returning. I pulled anxiously at the long grass and the thick weeds that grew around the foot of the wall, my fear escalating as the minutes passed and still there was no sign.

The possibility that he would not return was unbearable. He had to come back. He *had* to. I would see his face again and those amber eyes would gaze into mine and in the gold-flecked depths there would be joy and pleasure . . . and love.

In the brilliant sunlight something moved. I held my breath as the miniscule dot of a car sped out of the haze and down the road. Frantically I shielded my eyes, straining to see better. Like a toy the car sped between fields of waving grain and then onto the grassy plain that circled Cotanes. It was not a police car. The blood pounding in my ears I watched it as it turned off the road, beginning the long ascent to the village.

Slowly I rose to my feet, walking to the very edge of the road, standing there in my own private hell as I waited for Garmendia to sweep round the last bend.

Chapter Twenty-two

I felt sick and dizzy and had no idea of what I was going to do as the throb of his car engine sounded faintly in the distance. The note altered, vibrating on the air as he changed down gears, the sound coming steadily nearer and nearer. My eyes stung with unshed tears as I waited for him, my heart empty of anything, even of hate.

Then he was below me, forcing his car round the last tortuous bend and I stepped out into the road, my mouth dry and parched, my heart hammering.

The sun glittered on his windscreen, temporarily blinding me and then he swerved to avoid me, the car bonnet smashing into the loose stone of the decaying wall, missing me by only a couple of feet.

I didn't move. Couldn't move. And then as my heart turned a somersault I said weakly: "Romero. . . ."

He slammed the car door behind him, walking towards me. I sat down suddenly on the wall, my knees weak, my head in my hands, my cheeks wet with tears of relief.

"Alison," he said, and I wiped my tears away, lifting my head, saying thankfully:

"I thought it was Garmendia. . . ." and then I saw his face and my heart died within me.

He made no move towards me, simply stared at me with deadened eyes. I struggled to speak, my body bathed in sweat.

"Where . . . ?" I managed at last.

Romero said tonelessly. "There's a deep quarry about ten, twelve miles away. The grass at the roadside was flattened by tyre marks

... he must have been travelling very fast. The car was still burning. I couldn't get down to it ... but there was no point. The fire was dying out and I could see the remains of his body still at the wheel ..."

I turned my head, crying into the flower filled grass and then Romero put his arm around my shoulder, and leaving his car spread-eagled across the road, led me back to the inn, his shoulders hunched in grief and defeat.

The worst had happened as I had known it would. Jose was dead and I would never see him again. I remembered our last parting, when I had determindly kept my eyes averted from his, and the pain submerged me. Nothing mattered anymore. Somehow I would return to England, back to the office and to my life in London that I had never given one thought to in the past few days. It seemed impossible that so short a time could alter my life so drastically.

From now on, no matter how many people I was surrounded by, no matter how many friends I had, I would always be lonely. Without Jose I could be nothing else.

They stared at me, their faces white and shocked. Romero sat on a bar stool, staring down at the floor, his hands hanging loosely between his knees. Javier and Miss Daventry looked helplessly on, unable to offer any words of comfort, stunned into silence.

At last I said. "There is no point in staying here now."

"No, of course not," Miss Daventry said, rallying herself. "How many of us can get into the car, Romero. All of us?"

He nodded. "All except Cia. ...."

I had forgotten Alphonso Cia. Romero's voice was expressionless. Javier said. "Let the barman see to him when we have left. It is better for Cia that none of us go to him now."

Miss Daventry adjusted her hat slowly and wearily. "Come along, Alison. And Romero. It is time we left."

Dejectedly Romero slipped off his stool, putting his arm heavily round my shoulders as we began to walk to the door. It was Pedro who spoke. His gun was in his hand and he was pointing it at us, saying pleasantly. "No-one is leaving."

Incredulously Javier said. "Are you mad? The only person to come back here is Garmendia," and then, more surer. "You want to wait for Garmendia . . . to be revenged?"

Pedro shook his head. "I am sorry my friend," he said unregretfully. "You have not understood."

Miss Daventry gave a small cry, like an animal in pain, then said slowly in disbelief. "I understand Pedro. I wondered about it before . . . Garmendia wasn't in Miguelou when Father Calzada told us of the plan to take Luis and Jose back to Bayonne by sea. I assumed he'd been told of it . . . but he didn't need telling, did he? You knew of it, and it was *you* who warned the coastguards and the police about the rescue attempt in the bay. And in the war, it was the same, wasn't it?" she said, her voice shaking. "You played it safe then. I often wondered at your luck, Pedro. How you managed to recover so quickly from Guernica. The others lost everything, yet within months you had a new inn . . . a new boat. . . . What a heaven sent gift you must have been to the Nationalists. A staunch Basque Republican, suspected by no-one, willing to sell information about our defences or lack of them. . . ."

Pedro cut her off abruptly, saying to Javier: "Don't do it! It won't be you I'll shoot before you shoot me. It will be the girl."

Javier had his hand on his gun.

"*You son of a bitch!*" Javier hissed, tensing himself like an animal ready to spring on its prey.

Pedro said viciously. "Don't try any heroics. Simply get down those cellar steps and release Alphonso."

"*Never,*" Javier said, his eyes blazing. "You'll have to kill me first, Pedro Triana. And not in the back. While I'm stood here facing you!"

"All through the war . . ." Miss Daventry was still saying, ashen-faced and trembling.

"I made the right choice though, didn't I? We could never have won. I knew that. And I like to be on the winning side. Angel Garmendia is on the winning side. He means business. Villada is dead now. The local units will be re-grouped, re-organised. . . ."

Romero dived past me, knocking Pedro backwards and in the

same split second the gun went off. Romero was sprawled on the floor and Pedro, cursing and gasping for breath was raising himself up shakily, the gun still in his hand, pointed lethally towards us.

"Romero!" I cried, moving forward at the same time as Miss Daventry cried out:

"No, Alison. Don't move! He's alive . . . he didn't hit him!"

In grotesque slow motion, Romero heaved himself to his feet. Pedro's eyes, wild and uncertain, his face glistening with sweat, trying to keep us all covered, watching every movement.

"*You,*" he said to me, his eyes on Javier and Romero. "There's a knife behind the bar. Take it with you and free Alphonso. If you don't I'll shoot again. I mean it. Angel said to keep you all alive till he came back . . . but another false move and so help me, I'll kill every last one of you."

His eyes were glazed, the eyes of a madman. Slowly I walked past him to the bar. The barman had long since discreetly disappeared. The knife was there as he had said it was. Gingerly I picked it up and paused a second. Wild thoughts of spinning round, plunging it deep into Pedro's back, chased through my mind, but it wouldn't work. Even if I tried Pedro would still manage to kill one of the others. I opened the cellar door and stepped down into the darkness.

There was only the shaft of light from the opened door to see by and it took several seconds before my eyes became accustomed to the gloom and I could see. A shape, darker, more solid than the wine barrels that stacked the wall, was vaguely discernable only yards from where I stood.

I was beyond fear now. Emotionally exhausted, numbed into a stupor, I sawed through the rope that bound his hands behind his back, and at the rope tying his feet and knees. I had no need to unknot the rag that covered his mouth. He pulled it viciously away, cursing with pain as he tried to stand, rubbing his aching muscles and joints. Then, gripping my shoulder, he pushed me violently in front of him, my shins grazing against the cellar steps. As I fell he blasphemed angrily, pushing me again as I rose to my feet, sending me stumbling through the doorway, back into the airless room.

Romero was on his feet again, his face contorted with hatred and grief. Javier was still motionless, but the dazed look of disbelief had long since vanished.

Cia pushed me in the small of the back again with his fist, and I saw Javier's face tighten as I lurched into him. Pedro seemed relieved at having Cia's support. He handed him a gun and Cia said: "Where's Angel?"

"I don't know. But he won't be long. Villada is dead."

Alphonso didn't query it. One look at Romero's face was enough to satisfy him of the truth.

"Stay here while I go for a look."

It was obvious that Pedro would have preferred to be the one going for a look, but he didn't argue. Romero, Javier and myself stood helpless before him, and out of the corner of my eye I could see Miss Daventry, looking old and tired.

I remember thinking. He'll walk to the bend like I did, and watch for Garmendia's car approach just as I had watched for Jose's.

Romero said quietly. "Before this day is over Pedro Triana. I am going to kill you."

Pedro's geniality was getting a little ragged at the edges, but he managed a half-hearted smile and laugh.

"There will be no-one left to kill me. Not after Angel arrives."

I looked from Pedro's face to Romero's, and if I had been Pedro, gun or no gun, I would have been a frightened man.

Silence fell, thick with tension as the seconds lengthened into minutes and the minutes increased. Pedro was sweating hard, drips of perspiration running down his face.

Miss Daventry said: "And if it had been Garmendia dead and Jose who returned, I don't suppose we would ever have known the truth about you, would we, Pedro?"

He didn't bother to reply. There was no need. Running footsteps rang out over the cobbles and panting for breath Alphonso Cia burst into the bar, gasping: "I've seen him. He's on his way here!"

Relief was apparent on Pedro's face. It filled him with fresh optimism and his smile was no longer uncertain.

"Not long now," he said gloatingly to Romero. "And after you it will be your brother's turn. Luis."

He was mad, quite mad. The three of us stood like figures in a Greek tragedy, watching the shadows fall across the genial face, and his eyes grow more fevered.

Cia had swung back out, racing across the square to the bend once more, his running feet no longer within hearing.

"No chance of revenge now, Villada," Pedro said smugly.

The shot exploded in the small room, splitting the air, deafening our ears. Pedro screamed, reeling back, his gun falling to the floor, his hand hanging limply, blood pouring down his arm. He stared uncomprehendingly in those few split seconds as Miss Daventry stood, the gun Romero had given her earlier, smoking in her hand. Then Pedro dived down, still screaming and Miss Daventry was clutching frantically at Javier's arm, as he tried to take aim.

"*No Javier, No.* Don't face a murder charge for him!"

Romero had lurched forwards and Pedro jumped across him, leaping for the door and the street.

"Get Cia!" Romero yelled to Javier, flying out after Pedro, Miss Daventry, her battle with Javier won, hard at his heels. With a face of white-hot rage Javier raced out of the bar and across the square. Miss Daventry had gone, her straw hat firmly wedged on her head, camera and binoculars crosswise about her chest, tearing after Romero like a woman possessed.

Only the pool of Pedro's blood on the floor gave any indication of what had happened. I ran to the open door, but there was no-one in sight. From the left of me I could hear Romero's shouts and I turned, running in the direction of his voice. There was only one point in Cotanes higher than the square and that was up a dirt track that led behind the inn up to the village church. I could see Miss Daventry running as fast as she could and Romero several yards in front of her, and Pedro nearly at the church door. With a last backward glance for Javier, I plunged up the hillside after them.

Perhaps Pedro had turned upwards in the hope of finding a priest in the church. Perhaps there *was* a priest in the church. If so he would stand little chance of protecting Pedro against the raging Romero.

I raced on, my chest hurting me as the way steepened. Twice I fell, struggling back to my feet, my knees stained with grass, my hands dirty. The wooden church door was slammed shut as I gasped my way up to it, thrusting it open and running in.

My immediate surge of relief that the church was derelict and no innocent priest in danger, was tempered by the fact that Pedro, Romero and Miss Daventry had seemingly vanished into thin air.

"Romero . . ." I cried, dashing down the nave, "Romero. . . ."

The noises came from above my head. I halted, panting for breath, searching for the source of Romero's muffled voice. Beside what had once been the high altar, a door swung softly shut. I ran across to it, pulling it open. The spiralled stone steps wound narrowly upwards, sunlight pouring down on them from above. Romero was saying:

"I told you I would kill you Pedro Triana, and I meant it."

Miss Daventry was saying urgently. "Romero . . . no. . . ."

I raced up the stone steps, lurching out onto the perilous ledge of the bell tower. Pedro was facing Romero, his back to the drop behind him, his arm hung loosely. I dashed past Miss Daventry, grasping Romero's arm, saying: "For God's sake, no, Romero. He isn't worth it . . . he. . . ."

My words were lost on the man by my side. Without looking at me, he handed me his gun, pressing it into my palms. Then, unarmed, while Pedro's petrified eyes stared transfixed, he took a deliberate step forward.

"*No!*" Pedro screamed, backing away. "*No!* . . .

"You would kill Luis as well, would you Triana?"

"No! I didn't mean it! It was a mistake!"

"It was a mistake all right," Romero said, moving a step further forward.

Beside us the giant bell hung rusted on its heavy chain, creaking as the wind tugged at it. I kept my eyes firmly away from the vast drop. From the steep slopes of the towering bastion of rock on which Cotanes stood. From the dizzying distance of the plain far below.

"No!" Pedro screamed again, backing away. Then his foot slipped and his scream lengthened, rending the air as his outstretched arms flailed, mouth gaping, eyes wide, plummeting to the stony ground.

Chapter Twenty-three

For minutes Romero stood, poised on the very edge of the narrow parapet, gazing down at Pedro's broken body.

My breathing was slowly returning to normal and Miss Daventry grasped my hand in hers, saying tiredly: "It was best that it ended this way. No-one has his blood on their hands. He could have stepped forward and faced Romero. Romero was unarmed. He wouldn't have lived a day in Miguelou once the villagers knew of his treachery." She was thinking, I knew, of the civil war.

Grim-faced Romero took his gun from me and in single file we hurried down the narrow spiral of stone, into the cool dimness of the church. Romero began to run and Miss Daventry cried after him: "Where are you going?"

"For Cia," he shouted back over his shoulder, then he pushed the door open and was gone.

Miss Daventry raised her eyes heavenwards, re-arranged her camera and binoculars, took a deep breath and began to run down the nave towards the still open door.

"Miss Daventry ..." I called, but my efforts to stop her were useless. She paid no attention at all and by the time I reached the door was already twenty to thirty yards away, chasing down the hillside like a girl of twelve.

I had no desire to follow. Both Romero and Javier were armed and match enough for Alphonso Cia. I had had enough of death for one day. The afternoon sun was stiflingly hot, the breeze that stirred the long grass and weeds, merely a soft breath and nothing more. Below me I could see the rear of the inn and the still empty square. Shielding my eyes against the sun's glare I could see the bob of a straw boater as it hurried towards the bend and the road that led into Cotanes. If only she had left me the binoculars, I thought, straining to see more clearly. I held my breath, seeing the familiar figure of Romero run round the bend and out of sight.

I lowered my hand, intending to walk steadily down and meet them, but as I turned the corner of the church I sucked my breath in sharply.

Only yards away from me, sprawling bloodily and lifelessly, was the crumpled figure of Pedro. For a hasty moment I thought he was still moving, but it was only the scarf around his neck, blowing lightly in the air.

I hesitated, not knowing what to do. I couldn't just walk off and leave him like that ... I would have to stay there till Romero and Javier returned. Unwillingly I took a step towards him ... after all, Romero had not checked that he *was* dead. I fought a rising tide of nausea as I drew near enough to see his face, quickly turning my head away. One brief glance at his face, at the staring eye-balls, the blood matting his hair, the trickle of vomit at the side of his mouth, was enough. Pedro was dead as anyone can be.

I did not look at him again but walked away, over the grass to what had once been the churchyard, sitting gratefully down beneath the shade of a solitary oak tree. I could no longer see the inn from where I sat, but the dust-white road showed clearly as it left the village, sweeping in an arc, disappearing as it looped round the hillside, appearing again much further down before emerging at last on the flat plain of land that swept away into the distance. The green of pasture land merging into the pale gold of the cornfields. I closed my eyes, leaning my head against the mossy bark of the tree, the leaves rustling above my head giving me cooling shade.

It was as if in the last half hour I had been anaesthetised against my loss. Now I was coming round, the hurt of my grief raw and open. I unzipped my shoulderbag, lifting out the German Walther he had given me in the cottage and which I had kept ever since. It seemed too cruel that the only memento I should be left with, was an object as destructive as a gun. I pushed it out of sight, closing my bag.

The sun, still hot was beginning to shift to the west and the shadow of the tree was lengthening. There was still no sign of anyone returning and the parts of the road that I could see remained deserted. I closed my eyes again. They would be back soon, and whatever they decided to do with Pedro's body it would no longer be my responsibility. Until then I would stay here, unable to see it myself, but able to shoo away the children if they should venture anywhere near.

A bird called, plunging into the foliage above me and I was reminded of Lindaraja. Of Jose sitting up in the giant four-poster bed, hair tangled, eyes laughing, complaining none too seriously about the noise of the doves that cooed and fluttered outside his open window.

I would re-live again all the time we had together, committing it to memory so that not one second should be lost. In memory I was driving the car again, through the evening light towards the beach. Behind me the mountains rose, a shining escarpment of silver rock, shaded by the sinking sun so that their lower slopes appeared to be purple and lilac, merging into forests of glossy dark pines. My head nodded lower and I drifted off into sleep.

I was so exhausted, both physically and emotionally, that nothing stronger than the sound of a car engine would have awoken me. For an instant I gazed bewilderingly round, then saw the shabby black car cross the square and begin to crawl up the dirt-road towards me.

There was no sign of Romero or Javier. Or Miss Daventry. And sleep fled. I knew I had been too complacent in believing that all danger was over. It had never occurred to me that Cia would be any match for Romero and Javier. I had forgotten completely that Alphonso Cia had said Angel Garmendia was already approaching Cotanes ... and that was an age ago ... before Pedro had fled from the inn. With increasing horror I saw that the sun was sinking down in the pale glimmer of dusk and that the shadows had lengthened, the air cool with the first hint of the coming night.

I leapt to my feet, staring round frantically. Pedro's body had fallen down the left hand side of the church, out of sight of the rough track. But Garmendia must know it was there. He wouldn't be making the rough journey to the church just to see the view!

I was cornered with nowhere to hide. There was no way back down to the square and the inn without Garmendia seeing me. The only possible shelter was the tree.

I think, as I turned, that I had some wild idea of being able to climb it and hide amongst the stout branches and mass of leaves.

But the lowest branch was way above my head, the car was out of sight now as it crawled to a halt only yards away from me, round the corner of the church.

With a sob I pressed my back against the tree, holding my skirts in, vainly hoping that when he came round the corner looking for Pedro's body, the thick tree-trunk would hide me from view. It wasn't much of a hope but it was all I had.

I heard the car door slam and held my breath, elbows pressed in, trying to physically shrink in size . . . then I saw my bag. It lay in the grass only a yard away from me, but a yard that I dare not cross. And it held the gun.

What was it Jose had said to me? It holds nine bullets . . . and he had put a fresh magazine in when we had been at Lindaraja, and I had never used it since.

A minute passed, and then two, and still there were no soft footsteps on the grass. I let out my breath slowly, my panic subsiding, growing into something far more terrible. Growing into hate and the first tiny seeds of revenge.

I felt quite calm once I had made my mind up. He was inside the church, standing mere feet away, waiting for me to emerge from behind my inadequate hiding-place. Decisively I stepped away from the tree, bending low to the grass and unzipping my bag, and then, carefully and coolly, my palm grasped the gun and I withdrew it, leaving my bag where it was. I looked to see if it was ready to fire, and then, with no feeling of fear at all, I began to walk towards the door of the church. Softly I opened the door, softly I closed it behind me.

The waning rays of sunlight arrowed, dust-filled, onto the empty pews and the deserted nave. The door to the bell-tower was only vaguely discernible in the dimness, but I could see enough to know that it was closed. Other corners were too dark to see into. I waited silently, my ears straining to hear his footsteps or to catch the faint sound of breath other than my own.

The noise came sure enough . . . and it was from above, from the bell-tower. Softly I went up the aisle, pausing in front of the high altar, the door to the bell-tower still safely shut. I stepped back into the dark shadows, my eyes fixed on the door, the gun raised as Jose had told me how to. My gun arm straight, the left hand grasped around the wrist of the right, the pin at the back of the gun showing a bullet was in position and ready to fire, my reflexes ready to pull the trigger and swing the gun up in a smooth arc to avoid a vicious kick-back.

A mouse scuttled round the edge of a pew, disappearing into the gloom and motes of dust still danced, trapped in the bars of slanting light from the arched windows. I thought I heard him curse to himself, and then he was running lightly down the stone steps, taking no care to be silent. I steadied my breath, eyes straining to see the first opening of the door, hands quite firm.

The door opened and he stepped into the church, his breathing heavy and impatient. He still had on the blue tee-shirt he had been wearing when I had burst in on his conversation at the inn in Miguelou, the same red scarf tied around his neck. He leant back against the door as it closed and once again I was strongly aware that he was both impatient and angry. Before I moved again, I said flatly:

"Don't move or I'll shoot."

I was aware of his exclamation, of his suddenly turned head. I went on before I lost my nerve.

"I have every intention of shooting you Angel Garmendia, but before I do so I want the pleasure of telling you why." To my annoyance I heard a break in my voice. "You call yourself a Basque and a separatist when all you are is a murderer with no care for your country, or neighbours at all. For your egotistical lust of power you informed against your friends . . . even seeing your own brother killed because of you!"

He moved slightly and my voice rose up an octave. "Don't move! I mean it!" He remained motionless and I said: "And if that wasn't enough you and Pedro between you saw to it that the plans to rescue the Villada's failed, and cold bloodedly shot a policeman in order to frame Jose and myself. Well, now it's your turn to be afraid. And if you're not you should be. Because as sure as I'm standing here, I'm going to kill you. For Jaime's death. For Jose's death, and for countless others who's name I don't know."

He said gutturally: "You're English . . . what is this to you?"

"What is it to me!" I said, my voice breaking completely. "I'll tell you what it is to me. I don't know what happened at that quarry, but you killed Jose Villada. I don't believe, I simply *refuse* to believe, I will not *believe* that Jose crashed into that quarry accidentally. I . . . do . . . not . . . believe . . . it! And even if he had it would still be your fault," I added illogically.

"Villada! Why should you care about a rogue like Villada?"

"Because," I cried passionately. "I love him! And because of you he died without my ever even telling him. Without me even saying goodbye to him the last time we parted! And no matter how long I live I shall never me able to forget him or love anyone else and I hate you Angel Garmendia. I *hate you. I hate you.!*"

He took a step forward and I half closed my eyes, the gun pointing straight at his chest, my finger curling round the trigger.

"For God's sake put it down," my lover said. "You might just hit me."

I said stupidly: "*Jose!*"

He was out of the shadows now. The clothes he wore were Garmendia's, but the handsome face, the laughing eyes, were Jose's.

His arms were held out and I flung the gun aside and ran into them, my arms tightening unbelievingly around him, his heart thudding against my own. His lips on my hair, and as I turned my rapturous face to his, on my mouth.

Chapter Twenty-four

It was a long, long time later that we stepped out into the purple dusk of evening, his arm around my waist, my head on his shoulder. Fire-flies flew around us and instead of the sleepy scent of the wild roses and foxgloves that edged the path, the air seemed filled once more with the heady fragrance of musk and civet.

He said, holding me tightly to him. "I love you, how could you ever have doubted it?"

I was unable to answer as his lips kissed my hair, my eyes, my lips. He held my face between his hands. "Never doubt me again, little one."

"No," I said, my arms around him. "Never."

Our eyes met and we smiled slowly at each other. "Who would have thought," Jose said, gently teasing. "That the little English girl who was afraid to climb the mountain in the dark would threaten to shoot down a thug like Angel Garmendia?"

I took his hand away from my face, clasping it tightly as we continued down the darkening track. "I wasn't afraid." I said. "And I'm not little."

"You are to me," he said laughing, sweeping me up in his arms and running down to the corner where an oil lamp outside the inn cast a rosy glow across the square. He kissed me once more.

"Prepared to meet the rabble?" he asked.

I nodded, my arm snug around his waist as we stepped into the candle-lit interior. Romero was sat on a bar stool, back towards the zinc topped bar, a large glass of wine in his hand and a broad smile on his battered and bruised face as we entered. Javier gave a whoop of joy, leaping to his feet and kissing me enthusiastically despite Jose's protests.

Miss Daventry smiled with satisfaction. "How nice to see you again, Alison. I was beginning to think you were lost for good."

There was no sign of Alphonso Cia. Reading my thoughts Miss Daventry said pleasantly. "That bull-necked gentleman who commandeered the doorway earlier on was really quite nice once you got to know him. He has taken Cia down to the nearest hospital. His hand somehow got a bullet in it. Cleaning his gun and it went off I believe. At least that is what Alphonso will say if he ever hopes to live south of the Pyrannees again."

Javier patted his chest proudly. "I *could* have killed him if I had wanted to. But I decided to be compassionate. So all I did was to incapacitate his shooting for a little while. In fact I doubt if he will ever be able to shoot properly again!"

"Thank God you're shooting isn't as perfect as you claim, otherwise I'd be dead." Jose said with a grin. "When Garmendia ran from the inn he leapt into the police car, not his own. I understood it when I raced after him in his. He was nearly out of petrol."

"I didn't see," Miss Daventry said unnecessarily. "I just assumed that they would have raced off in the cars they arrived in. A logical conclusion I would have thought."

"And despite your convictions that the car couldn't possibly have ended up at the bottom of the quarry by mistake, that's exactly what did happen." Jose said, laughing down at me with a blaze of desire behind the smile that stirred my body, making my hand tighten over his.

"But if haring off after Garmendia was dangerous, it was nothing compared with getting back here! When Garmendia swerved off the road, pitching down into the quarry the car didn't set immediately on fire. I scrambled down to him . . . I could see he was unconscious and most likely dead, but I had to make sure. He was dead when I got to him, but there was still Cia to take care of. So I got the bright idea that nearly killed me! I took Garmendia's shirt and necktie, thinking that as I was driving Garmendia's car it would make it easy to fool Cia and get close to him. Well, as it happened

I didn't need to confuse Cia, Javier and Romero had taken care of him, but it certainly fooled these two idiots!"

"We fired on him," Javier said happily with a grin.

"But thanks to his aim which is nearly as bad as Alison's, he hit the tyre not the windscreen. . . ."

"And he went spinning off the road," Javier finished. "And at that time we had our hands full with Cia so we left Garmendia, as we thought, to struggle up the hill."

"I found him," Miss Daventry said triumphantly. "Climbing up the hillside under what cover he could get. . . ."

"And very glad I was to see you," Jose said, putting his arm around her shoulders. "If it had been either of those two idiots I would never have lived to tell the tale!"

"Binoculars you see," Miss Daventry said brightly. "I never go anywhere without them. I knew they would come in useful one day. I could see it was your face and not Angel's from miles away."

"And then when I finally make it, and go rushing all over the countryside for you," Jose said, turning to me. "What happens? You came within a hairs breadth of shooting me down yourself. I'll tell you something," he said, grinning at Javier and Romero. "I would rather have Alison for me than against me any day!"

"What are we going to do about Pedro?" I asked, remembering the grotesque body outside the church.

"We are about to remove it. Now." Javier said. "And Milo is lending me another car to take it away and dispose of it suitably."

"Milo?"

"The barman."

I stared unbelievingly from him to the barman. He was still polishing his glasses. His face never slipped into even the remotest of smiles, but he winked slowly with one eye and then concentrated once more on what he was doing.

"Oh," I said, and Miss Daventry patted my hand.

"I've had a word with him," she said in explanation. "And I'm going to help Javier and Romero. You and Jose can travel back to Bayonne by yourselves," and they all trooped past us towards the door. The candle on the table flickered and in the soft light Jose's eyes met mine, deepening with desire and love."

"There can be no returning to Spain," he said huskily. "But there is Argentina . . . and the horses. I was there for ten years, the land is still mine."

"Solitaire?" I asked, held closely in the circle of his arms.

"A wedding present, if you will have me, little one."

"Forever and ever, Jose."

"Forever," he said, his lips coming down on mine, "will not be long enough!"

www.ingramcontent.com/pod-product-compliance
Ingram Content Group UK Ltd.
Pitfield, Milton Keynes, MK11 3LW, UK
UKHW040640280225
455688UK00002B/23